REA

ELEMENTARY, MY DEAR

groucho

Other Groucho Marx Mysteries

Groucho Marx, Master Detective
Groucho Marx, Private Eye

ELEMENTARY, MY DEAR groucho

Ron Goulart

Thomas Dunne Books
St. Martin's Minotaur
New York

THOMAS DUNNE BOOKS.
An imprint of St. Martin's Press.

Production Editor: David Stanford Burr

Library of Congress Cataloging-in-Publication Data

Goulart, Ron.
　　　Elementary, my dear Groucho / Ron Goulart. — 1st ed.
　　　　　p.　cm.
　　　"Thomas Dunne books."
　　　ISBN 0-312-20892-8
　　　1. Marx, Groucho. 1891–1977 Fiction.　I. Title
　　PS3557.O85E44　　　1999
　　813'.54—dc21　　　　　　　　　　　　　　99–33991
　　　　　　　　　　　　　　　　　　　　　　　　CIP

First Edition: November 1999

10　9　8　7　6　5　4　3　2　1

To Walt Truett Anderson, Piet Goedewaagen, and
Terry Wollter, companions of my youth

Acknowledgments

Once again my thanks to Robert Finkelstein for his cooperation. And to Ruth Cavin and Marika Rohn for their continuing interest.

ELEMENTARY, MY DEAR groucho

One

It was shortly before Christmas of 1938 that Groucho Marx matched wits with Sherlock Holmes.

The whole business began as an ill-advised Hollywood publicity stunt, but before everything was over Groucho and I became a detective team again and found ourselves involved in trying to solve a couple of murders.

"This detective stuff is all well and good," Groucho had conceded, "but the next time you get me on a team, see if you can make it the Los Angeles Angels. I just know I'd make a delightful shortstop. I've already had several years experience as a doorstop, but that's not as good exercise."

We initially got tangled up with the case early on a Tuesday morning in December. It was one of those gray, blurry Los Angeles days, overcast and not quite warm enough. A few stray seagulls were circling up in the morning mist, intermittently visible, their mournful cries muffled.

I was driving and Groucho was sitting, slightly slouched, in the passenger seat of my new Ford sedan. He was quietly singing "Jeepers Creepers" in a very bad Swedish accent and keeping time on the dashboard with his unlit cigar. "This vehicle is a considerable improvement over your late Plymouth coupe," he observed, inserting the cigar between his teeth. "Though I really miss that raccoon tail you used to fly from your radio antenna, Franklin."

I'm Frank Denby, by the way, and I'd been writing Groucho's comedy detective show for radio. That, however, had been canceled back in October and right at the moment we were collaborating on a script for a screwball movie comedy. It was about a poor girl who inherits a bus line and the tentative title was *Cinderella on Wheels*. We were driving, on that overcast morning, out to the Mammoth Studios in the valley to talk to a producer about our idea.

And let me mention here, for those of you who've been following these accounts, that I'd been married since June to Jane Danner, America's best-looking cartoonist. Groucho had served as our best man and also volunteered to sing "Oh, Promise Me" at the ceremonies. We'd allowed him to do that only after he'd promised he wouldn't accompany himself on his guitar nor throw in the yodels he'd been inserting during the wedding rehearsals.

While my career was momentarily floundering, Jane was doing swell. She'd sold her *Hollywood Molly* comic strip in September and as the end of the year approached her syndicate had succeeded in placing it in just under 150 newspapers around the country. Her salary had climbed to seven hundred dollars a week. She'd already earned enough to buy us this new car in addition to a new bicycle for herself.

"I sure hope we sell this damn script," I said to Groucho as we neared the Mammoth Studios spread. "I'm enlightened enough to be able to live off my wife's income for a short spell, but I'd feel a hell of a lot better if my own funds weren't hovering near zero."

"Look on the bright side, Rollo," advised Groucho, fishing a book of Trocadero matches out of the pocket of his exuberantly plaid sports coat but making no effort to light his dead cigar. "As long as you're a kept man, it's nice that you're being kept by such a bright, attractive young lady as Jane. Now, the last woman who kept me insisted on keeping me in a very cramped duffel bag. What with me, my salt and pepper shaker collection, and all those stray duffels in there, it was far from roomy. It was, in point of fact, nearly seventy-seven hot, weary miles from roomy and up hill all the way."

A pair of workmen in coveralls were on a scaffold putting up a new billboard on the high white stucco wall that surrounded the fifteen acres that Mammoth covered. The headline of the big poster read: *Miles Ravenshaw IS Sherlock Holmes in Mammoth Pictures' Production of THE VALLEY OF FEAR!* The top third of Ravenshaw had already been slapped up and you could see his deerstalker cap, his meerschaum pipe, and a profile that suggested that he believed whoever it was who'd once told him that he looked a lot like John Barrymore.

"Miles Ravenshaw," muttered Groucho as I guided the car up to the gilded wrought-iron studio gates. "I'd call him a ham, except that would be an insult to all the self-sacrificing pigs who donated their backsides so that the world could have ham on rye."

"They say that Ravenshaw was a Scotland Yard inspector before he became an actor."

Groucho expressed his disbelief with a rude noise. "Of course, for religious reasons I can't have anything to do with a ham of any sort," he said. "I'm even forbidden to drop in on the Three Little Pigs, nor can I so much as huff and puff and blow any of their houses down." He waggled his unlit cigar. "I'm sorely tempted to mention an attractive miss I once encountered in a Baja California bordello who could not only huff and buff but . . . but, no, some things are best left unsaid."

I stopped a few feet from the closed gates. "That'd make a good motto for you," I suggested.

"It would indeed, Rollo, and I may well use it in my forthcoming B movie, *Think Fast, Mr. Motto*."

Just outside the gates was a tile-roofed guard shack with a single palm tree rising up beside it. A plump uniformed guard in a dark gray uniform came shuffling out and walked over to the car, his hand resting casually on the holster at his right side. "How can I help you, gents?" he inquired, looking in at Groucho.

"I'm deeply hurt, Oscar," said Groucho. "After we served three years in the Foreign Legion together, I hoped you'd never forget me."

The heavyset Oscar chuckled, shaking his head. "Sorry, I didn't recognize you right off, Mr. Marx," he told him. "You know, because you don't have your mustache."

"I don't?" He touched his fingertips to his upper lip, then turned to scowl at me. "As soon as we send for a matron, Rollo, you'll be thoroughly searched. Mustache snatching is a serious thing and, if my vast knowledge of the law doesn't play me false, I am almost certain it's a capital crime. It may well also be the capital of North Dakota, but we won't be certain of that until the returns come in from the outlying provinces. Lord knows how long that'll take, since they've been out lying with . . . but, enough. You get my point, I'm sure."

4

Oscar took off his visored cap to scratch at his thinning blond hair. "I hear your last movie was a flop, Mr. Marx."

"You *hear*? *Didn't you have the nerve to go see Room Service?*"

"Well, I'd like to see all your Marx Brothers pictures," he assured Groucho, "but my wife just can't stand you. In her opinion you never play anything but a sex-crazed lecher in any of your movies."

"That's because I am a sex-crazed lecher," he responded. "But I'm struggling to make a living despite such a handicap. Isn't that the American way? Yes, a man may work to overcome his handicaps and make a name for himself. The name I wanted to make for myself was Edgar Rice Burroughs, but they told me it was already taken. I then selected Tarzan and it turned out some nudist over at MGM had dibs on that. Groucho Marx was just about all that was left, except for the Marx of Zorro and I thought that sounded too foreign for an actor who specializes in playing ice-skating ingenue parts."

"We've got an appointment with Lew Marker," I told the chuckling guard.

"Lew Number Two, huh?" The guard shrugged and shook his head. "Somebody of your stature, Mr. Marx, ought to be seeing Lew Number One."

Lew Goldstein, the head of the whole Mammoth operation, everybody called Lew Number One. Marker had the nickname Lew Number Two.

"I'm working my way up the ladder," Groucho assured Oscar. "Why only last year I wasn't able to see anybody higher than Lew Number Four-oh-six."

Chuckling once more, he said, "Park in Visitors' Lot A, folks," and went trotting back to his hut.

A moment later the gates shivered and then rattled open inward.

Giving the guard a lazy salute, I drove onto the studio grounds.

"I don't think all that much of Lew Marker myself," admitted Groucho. "Yet my esteemed brother, Zeppo, assures me that the fellow is greatly interested in talking to us about *Cinderella on Wheels.*"

The buildings were all of the popular cream-colored stucco and red tile roof school. There were several stretches of bright green lawn and rows of assorted kinds of palm trees. "Marker's produced a string of screwball comedies," I reminded him, stopping to let a starlet decked out as an aviatrix cross the street. "*Crazy About You, This One's on Me, That Was My Wife.* Irene Dunne came near getting an Academy Award nomination for one of them."

"The best of the bunch," said Groucho, lighting the cigar and exhaling smoke, "contained, and I'm quoting an exhaustive study conducted by the Greenwich Observatory, five laughs during its entire length. And the heartiest one came when the audience read the name of the musical director in the opening credits."

My Ford looked to be the least expensive car in the row I parked in, possibly the least expensive in the whole damn lot.

When I mentioned that to Groucho, he said, "True, but you have the curliest hair."

"My hair isn't curly at all."

"Well, gee, Penrod, you don't have to bite a guy's head off when he's only trying to cheer you up."

We were scheduled to meet Marker over at Soundstage 4,

where he was going to be sitting in on the shooting of scenes for his latest comedy, *She Married the Butler.*

We never made the appointment.

As we were walking past Soundstage 2, the big metal door slid open with a clattering bang. A pretty blond young woman came running out, pale under her tennis court tan.

She was wearing white slacks and a dark blue cable-stitch pullover sweater. "In there," she called to us, waving her hand in the direction of the doorway she'd just come stumbling through. "A dead man."

"We could, Rollo," suggested Groucho, "continue on our way and ignore this entirely."

"But we won't," I said, running toward the frightened girl.

Two

The blonde thrust both her slim arms around me, pressing hard against my ribs, then leaned her head against my chest. "They shot him," she murmured in a low, choked voice. "He's all bloody."

"Are *they* still in there?" I asked as I pushed her, gently, back a foot or so from me and nodded at the open doorway of the shadowy soundstage.

"He's dead. I'm certain he's dead." Her hand was shaking as she brought it up to brush a tangle of blond hair back from her forehead. "I came looking for him, you know, because he wasn't in his office and I had to ask him something about the script revisions. Somebody's shot him. I don't know who."

Putting both hands on the shivering woman's shoulders, I said, "Take it easy now. Tell me who it is that's dead."

She straightened up some, looking into my face. Her mascara had run from the crying and her eyes were underscored with sooty blurs. "Do you work here at the studio?"

"Although noted far and wide for my patience and stoicism," said Groucho, moving closer, "I would like to know when it's going to be my turn to get hugged?"

"Oh, it's you, Mr. Marx," said the young woman. "You probably don't remember me, but I used to be a script girl at MGM back when you were still active in the movies."

"Somebody else who missed seeing *Room Service.*" He slipped out of his flamboyant sports coat, shimmying quite a bit in the process, and draped it over the shivering girl's shoulders. "The important thing for a shock victim is to keep warm. That's a little something I learned during my years as a den mother with the Brownies. Soon as the Saint Bernard shows up, we'll give you a slug of brandy."

I asked him, "You know her?"

"Whilst trotting over here, I reflected to myself that the rear view was deucedly familiar." He shrugged. "Alas, the name escapes me."

"I'm Isobel Glidden." She was shivering less. "I've been a script girl here at Mammoth for close to a year, Mr. Marx."

"Don't be so formal, my dear. You can call me Hopalong."

"Okay, Isobel," I said, "Let's get back to this dead man— do you know who it is?"

"Yes, of course." When she nodded, Groucho's jacket started to slip down off her right shoulder. "It's Mr. Denker."

"Would that be Felix Denker," asked Groucho as he rearranged the coat, "the noted émigré director?"

"Yes, he's got a three-picture contract with the studio."

"I ran into him quite a few times at Anti-Nazi League festivities, Rollo," Groucho told me. "I admired his political stand, even though I thought Denker himself was an unmitigated putz and a pain in the tokus." He puffed on his cigar. "But I suppose it's not polite to speak too ill of the dead. So cancel the putz part of that remark."

10

Pointing a thumb at the wide doorway, I suggested, "We'd better go take a look."

Groucho patted Isobel on her lower back. "Are you capable of guiding us, my child?"

"I think so, yes," she said. "I really have to go back there eventually anyway. I dropped my script on the set when I saw him sitting there dead."

The dead man was sitting stiffly in Sherlock Holmes's armchair in the study at 221B Baker Street. He was tilted to the left in the velvet chair, his rigid left arm hovering over the small stack of early twentieth-century magazines that were scattered on the end table.

Felix Denker, a lean man in his middle fifties, had been shot twice on the upper right side of his chest. His twisted ascot and the front of his cream-colored silk shirt were splotched with dark, dried blood. His black hair was still neatly parted in the middle and slicked down, but his monocle had fallen to the floor of the set and lay on the white bearskin rug. There was no sign of a gun.

With Isobel's help, we'd located the control panels and turned on sufficient lights.

Careful not to disturb anything too much, I'd approached the body of the murdered director. Judging by the progress of rigor mortis, I figured he'd been shot several hours earlier. "Looks like he's been dead since last night," I said. "When'd you see Denker last, Isobel?"

She'd remained at the edge of the set, her reclaimed script clutched tightly to her chest with both hands. "Well, when I left the studio yesterday evening at around six, Mr. Denker was still in his office in the Directors Building."

Groucho was wandering around in the simulation of Holmes's lodgings. "I assume Felix was directing *The Valley of Fear*?" he asked the blonde.

"Yes, and he hated it."

"Having to work with Miles Ravenshaw would give anybody the heebie-jeebies." Groucho leaned over to peek into the microscope that rested on the chemistry bench in the corner. "How'd Little Egypt get in there?"

"He and Mr. Ravenshaw were continually squabbling, sure, but that wasn't what upset him," explained Isobel, trying to look at Groucho without looking at the corpse. "Mammoth had pretty much promised Mr. Denker that he'd be directing only quality films, but then they stuck him with a mystery. His first American film, *Lynch Mob*, was nominated for an Oscar in 1936, you know."

"Yes indeedy, Felix had mentioned that fact to me on more than one occasion." Groucho was inspecting the pipe rack on the set wall. "It always annoyed him when I stoutly insisted that I'd once seen a Walt Disney Silly Symphony with the same title as his masterpiece."

"Was he shooting the Holmes movie here last night?" I asked Isobel.

"No, we did only outdoor stuff yesterday over at the London standing set." She frowned. "We weren't due to use this set until this afternoon. I only tried hunting for him here because he had a habit of looking over the day's sets by himself sometimes."

"So he might've dropped in here last night to do that?"

"I suppose, yes."

"That's odd." Groucho was crouched next to Denker's body, eyeing his stiff left hand. "Forefinger's bloody."

There was dried blood thick on the dead director's finger. "Hey, it looks like he scrawled something on the cover of that magazine."

The top magazine was a prop copy of *The Strand* from 1915. Up just under the logo Denker had apparently started to write something on the pale cover, using his own blood for ink.

"Appears to be the number four," concluded Groucho, squinting.

It did look like an open-topped numeral four. "A dying message, maybe?" I glanced over at the script girl. "Four mean anything?"

Isobel shook her head. "It could mean just about anything," she pointed out. "Part of a phone number, you know, or an address, or a page number—and isn't there a Sherlock Holmes story with four in the title?"

"Dying messages always annoy me." Groucho straightened up, with a slight creak, still looking at what the dead man had written on the cover. "Victims in B movies are always penning cryptic phrases in ancient Persian or gasping out a snatch of lyric from a fifteenth-century madrigal to give the sleuths a hint as to who did them in." He paused to puff on his cigar. "Much simpler, in my opinion, if you just dashed off something like 'I was knocked off by Erwin L. Hershman of Twenty-six-B Sycamore Lane in Pismo Beach.' Or 'My wife's lover—I mean, the lout with the tattoo—did this, officers. It's my guess they're shacked up at this very moment in the Starcross Motel in Anaheim. Go get 'em.' "

I took a look around the set, tapping my fingers on Holmes's

Stradivarius that rested on a table near the door. "Well, I guess we'd better alert the security people about this," I said, "and they can call the local cops."

"Exactly, Rollo. There's absolutely no need whatsoever for us to get any further involved." Groucho was slouched in the chair that Dr. Watson usually occupied, gazing up into the crosshatch of catwalks and dangling lights high above us. "We'll do our civic duty, pause only long enough to pose for a few flattering photos for the gentlemen of the press, then journey on to our appointment with Lew Marker."

"I hope," said Isobel quietly, sniffling, "these things don't really come in threes."

Groucho popped to his feet. "What's that, Izzy?"

I asked, "Somebody else has been murdered?"

"Oh, it wasn't a murder," she answered. "But, you know, I can't help wondering if this darn movie isn't jinxed."

"Details, dear child, provide us with some details," Groucho requested, easing in bent-leg strides toward her.

Isobel rubbed at her nose with her thumb. "Well, Mr. Marx, it was only five days ago that Marsha Tederow got killed," she explained. "She was an assistant art director here at Mammoth and was working with Mr. Denker on *The Valley of Fear.*" She gestured in a vaguely northerly direction. "It was really awful—car accident way up on Mulholland someplace. Her coupe went off the road and down into a gully. It exploded and . . . Marsha was only twenty-seven and very attractive."

Narrowing my left eye and nodding at Groucho, I said, "A coincidence?"

"It makes no never mind, Mother Westwind," he told me. "What you're doing is letting these Holmesian surroundings affect your impressionable young brain. Although we performed brilliantly as amateur sleuths on a few memorable occasions in the past, we are not on the premises today in that capacity. No, I'm here, Mr. Anthony, simply to sign a contract to coauthor *Cinderella on Wheels* and then reap the huge financial rewards that Movietown bestows upon its truly gifted writers. While I'm at it, I might reap a few acres of alfalfa, too, but only so it'll distract the farmhands and keep them from dallying with my daughters. For, as Salvador Dalí so wisely put it when he was halfway through a six-day bike race and realized he had neglected to bring his bicycle, 'Six time six is thirty-six except in months that begin with a letter of the alphabet.' "

"That's a cute title," said Isobel.

"What's a cute title—Salvador Dalí?"

"No, I mean *Cinderella on Wheels*."

"We already registered it with the Screen Writers Guild, sister, so beware," he warned as he lurched closer to her.

I said, "Let's find a telephone, so we—"

"Would you folks mind putting up your hands?" inquired a voice off in the shadows beyond 221B.

Three

Jane asked me, "This is a serious conversation we're having? Not another sample of your kidding?"

I was in a dim-lit section of the big soundstage, slumped in a canvas chair, using the first phone I'd been able to locate. "I'm being absolutely truthful, sweetheart," I assured my wife. "We found Felix Denker in—"

"He's the German fellow who directed *The Confessions of Dr. Medusa* just before he fled Berlin in 1934, isn't he?"

"He's that Felix Denker, yes. For a while Groucho and I thought it was the Felix Denker who'd invented peanut butter, but a quick check of his identification papers proved we were in error," I said. "Anyway, my love, after we looked over the scene of the crime—"

"You've taken to saying *my love* exactly the way Groucho does."

"Look, Jane, I just came close to being arrested for murder, so I'm not especially in the mood for tips on elocution."

"You're absolutely right, darling," she said. "Besides, I have to learn to resign myself to the fact that I married a hopeless wiseass. Who tried to arrest you?"

"Fortunately it was only a security guard," I continued. "He was passing this soundstage and noticed the door wide open. He came in to look around and spotted Groucho and me and Isobel in the vicinity of the corpse."

"Isobel? Who might she be?"

"She works here at Mammoth as a script girl and she's actually the one who first found Denker's body," I explained. "She was pretty upset and happened to come running out of the soundstage looking for help just as Groucho and I were passing on our way to meet Marker."

"So you haven't seen him yet?"

"We've been detained here and won't be able to see Marker until this afternoon," I told her. "Did I mention Felix Denker was directing a Sherlock Holmes movie and his body's sitting in Holmes's favorite chair?"

"That's probably too obvious to be ironic," she said. "Was he shot there or just dumped?"

"I'd say, from the look of things, that he was shot right where we found him."

"Are you and Groucho going to be investigating this one, Frank?"

"Nope, no, not at all," I said firmly. "It was pure chance we got tangled up in this mess at all. See, Jane, after the first guard spotted us and pulled his gun—well, then he called in three other guards. They eventually accepted the fact that he was Groucho Marx, even though he doesn't appear in civilian life with his greasepaint mustache. So the consensus at the moment is that we probably aren't murderers, but we have to stick around until the police arrive and talk to us."

"I have this feeling you won't be home for lunch."

"Let's try for dinner," I suggested. "Anything new?"

"Well, as a matter of fact, yes," she told me, sounding happy. "I just heard from the syndicate and *Hollywood Molly* has picked up twenty more newspapers. Including—and I think that's great—the *San Francisco Chronicle.*"

"Keep this up and I'll never have to work again."

"You really aren't upset by the fact that I happen to be earning more than you are at the moment?" she asked me.

"Not at all," I said, trying to sound convincing. "Oh, and there was one other thing I wanted to tell you."

"Okay, what?"

"Now, what the heck was it?"

From out of the shadows stepped a uniformed policeman. He was tall and heavyset and he made a sour face at me, beckoning.

"Frank?" said my wife.

"I'm being summoned by the law," I said. "But I just remembered what I wanted to say: I love you."

"I was about to say the same," Jane said. "Don't get arrested, okay? And when you arrive home we can celebrate the twenty new papers. If you'd like."

"I would, yeah. Bye." I hung up the phone and stood to follow the cop.

"Young love," he muttered, making his way over a scatter of wires and cables. "It's downright touching."

Sergeant Jack Norment of the Burbank police was sitting on the edge of Sherlock Holmes's unmade bed. He was a middle-sized man, on the plump side, and about forty. I first met him back when I was on the police beat with the *Los Angeles Times.* Norment had a fondness for booze and always gave off a whiskey aroma, but he never seemed to be actually drunk. He was fairly honest, by Southern California cop standards.

The Holmes bedroom set was about fifty yards from the study. Over there a forensic crew and a medical team were going over the scene of the crime and the body of Felix Denker.

Norment had just finished questioning Isobel Glidden and told her she could leave.

Still upset, she took Groucho's sports coat off her shoulders and returned it to him. "Thanks, Mr. Marx," she said, giving him a quick kiss on the cheek before she left.

"Aw, gorsh, not in front of all the fellers, Izzy," he said.

"I admire your capacity to play the fool even under such unpleasant circumstances," said the sergeant with what looked to me like a mirthless smile.

"If you think this is unpleasant, Sarge, you should've seen the audience we played once in Pittsburgh." Groucho rose up out of the wicker armchair he'd been slouched in and started struggling into his coat. "They could never use the vaudeville house for a theater again because of the aura we left behind. They converted it into a funeral parlor. But even that didn't help, because people complained it was too gloomy."

"Should I write all this down?" Detective Ernie Sales was leaning at the edge of the bedroom set. He was a lanky, soft-spoken man who, he'd mentioned earlier, had never seen a Marx Brothers movie in his life so far. He was holding an open steno book and a gnawed yellow pencil.

"Use your own judgment," advised Norment.

"If Pittsburgh is too tough to spell, I can move the theater to Altoona," offered Groucho as he settled back into the chair.

Sergeant Norment fetched a pack of Camels out of a pocket in his rumpled suit coat. "It's gratifying to have a jester such

20

as yourself to question, Marx. Usually at a murder scene we get only grieving relatives and surly suspects."

"If you want to see grieving relatives, you can drop by my place any weeknight. Every time my wife realizes what a scoundrel she was hoodwinked into marrying, she breaks down and sobs. My two offspring, when not weeping into their gruel, spend all their time going over hospital records in the vain hope they can prove I'm not related to them in any significant way."

"You knew Denker?" Norment asked him.

"For the past two years or so," answered Groucho. "I met him and his wife, Erika Klein, at a rally staged by the Anti-Nazi League."

"You saw them socially?"

Shaking his head, Groucho answered, "Even though they both shared my views of Hitler and what he's doing to Europe, I didn't much like them."

"But you got along with Denker?"

Groucho left his chair, snatched out his book of Trocadero matches, and provided a light for the cigarette the policeman had just popped between his lips. "As I understand it, Sarge, Denker was shuffled off last night sometime." He wandered over to the cabinet that held Holmes's disguises. "Frank and I stumbled on the body this morning around ten and that's absolutely the only connection we have with this murder. As the young lady informed you, she was the one who first spotted the corpse. And running into a spotted corpse can be very unsettling, although there are those who favor candy-striped—"

"You didn't see anyone else here on the soundstage, Marx? Or anyone else leaving the place?"

"Not a soul." He locked both hands behind his back,

hunched, and scanned the disguises hanging in the open cabinet. "I wonder how I'd look in this Dutch-boy bob?"

Norment was smiling his unhappy smile again. "You used to be a pretty good reporter, Frank."

"Meaning I've fallen from grace since becoming a scriptwriter?"

"Meaning did you notice anything that Marx missed?"

"Nothing you and your guys haven't noticed, Jack," I answered. "Denker was shot at close range and there doesn't look to have been a struggle. Except for the bullet holes he wasn't mussed up at all. I'd estimate he was killed last night about eight or nine, but that's obviously a very rough guess. I think he was shot in the chair we found him in, not moved there from someplace else. Examining the armchair and checking the way the blood's settled in the corpse will probably confirm that."

Puffing on his cigarette, Norment flicked ashes on Sherlock Holmes's Persian carpet. "You think he was attempting to convey anything by what he appears to have scrawled on that old magazine?"

I answered, "If that's his own blood on his fingertip, it's a possibility."

"Maybe somebody else dipped Denker's finger into his wound and scrawled that shaky four just to divert us."

"Maybe King George V doodled part of one of his mistresses' phone numbers on that copy of *The Strand* and, after surviving the sinking of the *Titanic*, it found its way to a quaint secondhand magazine shop in Santa Monica until a prop man from—"

"If that is a four," Norment asked me, ignoring Groucho,

"and if the director did actually put it there, does it suggest anything to you?"

"Not a hell of a lot, Jack."

"Are you guys here playing private detective again?" asked Sales, looking up from his notebook.

"We visited this mecca of the cinematic arts for one reason only, my good man," said Groucho, taking a shaggy beard out of the cabinet and holding it up to the light from overhead. "We are interested solely in peddling a script. Later on, I have to concede, we may take time out to pedal Madeline home. But that's going to depend on—"

"I want to see him, damn you," shouted a woman's voice from the vicinity of the study set. "He's my husband, you stupid oaf."

"The grieving widow," observed Groucho, swinging the beard from side to side a couple of times.

Erika Klein also worked for the Mammoth studios. She'd been a professor of history before she and Denker had to get out of Germany. For nearly two years she'd been working at the studio as the head of their Historical Research Department. Supposedly she'd also been instrumental in getting the director his contract with Lew Goldstein.

"I just found out that poor Felix has been slain," Erika was shouting. "Let me see his body, please!"

Norment nodded at Sales. "Go curtail the lady, Ernie," he suggested. "Escort her to a quiet spot and muzzle her sorrow. I'll be over to chat with her in a short while."

Shutting his notebook, the plainclothes detective departed.

Norment turned to Groucho. "In some circles, unfortunately, it isn't too popular to be openly opposed to Hitler and the Nazis. Anybody you know of—say somebody who's active in the local German American Bund—ever threatened Denker or his wife?"

"Not at any of the political meetings or rallies that I've attended, no." Groucho hung up the beard. "Denker wasn't an especially likable fellow—something of a roadshow Fritz Lang. But if they started bumping off every unlikable director in town, the studios would have to shut down."

"Okay, what about Erika Klein's relationship with her husband? Did they get along well?"

"Every time I snuck over to their place, stood in the tulip beds, and peeked into their bedroom window, Sarge, they appeared to be getting along famously."

"Okay, you can both go." Norment gave us another of his humorless smiles and nodded at the way out. "You sure you aren't going to try to investigate this mess, Frank?"

"We aren't, nope," I assured the sergeant.

I believed it at the time.

We were nearing the doorway leading out of the shadowy soundstage when a policeman somewhere behind us shouted, "Hey, Sergeant, it's another body!"

Stopping still, Groucho said, "Dagnab it, Rollo, if that don't get my curiosity up."

"We just vowed not to get involved in this mess," I reminded him.

"I once took a vow of chastity." Pivoting, he started back the way we'd come.

Sergeant Norment, skirting cables and equipment, was

making his way toward another small set. As we caught up with him, more lights came on and the London pub became much easier to see into.

A uniformed cop and a plainclothesman were standing next to one of the three small tables on the wooden public house floor. Slumped at the table, her head next to a tipped-over beer mug and her fat arms dangling, was a heavyset woman. Her short-cropped hair was an unbelievable black and she was wearing a very rumpled navy blue suit.

The plainclothes policeman straightened up, stepping back and shaking his head. "False alarm, Jack," he said. "She's only passed out drunk."

"My fault," said the cop in uniform. "She looked dead when I first spotted her, Sergeant."

Norment stopped beside the unconscious woman. "Be nice to know who she is and why she went to sleep a few hundred yards from our corpse. Any sign of a purse?"

"Nope, and she's not carrying any identification."

I stepped onto the set. "I know who she is."

Frowning at me, Norment said, "Am I wrong, or didn't I already send you home, Frank?"

"We thought there was a national emergency." Groucho came over, leaned an elbow on the dark wood bar, and planted a foot on the short brass rail. "We rushed back to volunteer our services."

"Shall I give these guys the bum's rush?" asked the uniformed man.

"Nothing so fancy," said Groucho.

"You know this dame?" Sergeant Norment asked me. "Siegel, go get a medic to take a look at her."

25

Nodding, the cop left the pub.

I pointed at the loudly snoring woman. "She's Clair Rickson, a writer here at the studio."

"Why in the hell do we find her sozzled on this set?"

"Well, I think I heard she wrote the script for *The Valley of Fear.*" Standing this close to the sergeant, I noticed that he smelled more like a pub than the set did. "Although that doesn't exactly explain why she happens to be dead drunk at this particular location."

"The lady," added Groucho, "is noted for having been found drunk at any number of choice locations."

Clair Rickson, whom I'd met at a few gatherings of writers over the past couple of years, was in her middle forties. Born in Kansas someplace, she'd lived in Europe in the 1920s and early 1930s and been buddies with the likes of Gertrude Stein, Ernest Hemingway, and F. Scott Fizgerald. For the past few years she'd made a pretty good living with a series of hard-boiled, whimsical, and boozy mystery novels about a tough Hollywood lawyer named Jack Muldoon. Two of the novels, *The Case of the Cockeyed Carhop* and *The Case of the Jilted Jitterbug,* had been turned into successful programmers by Mammoth. Pat O'Brien had been borrowed from the Warner Brothers to play Muldoon.

Seating himself at the table, Norment studied the slumped author. "We have to find out how long she's been here," he said to the plainclothesman. "And what she may've seen and heard."

"And," added the cop, "if she's the one who shot that director."

I said quietly, "She's the sort of woman who only hurts herself."

Pushing back from the table, Sergeant Norment stood up. "Frank, thanks for helping me determine who this is," he said. "Once again I'd like to invite you and Groucho to scram."

"You're certain," asked Groucho, who'd wandered over to stare at the dartboard on the pub wall, "we can't help you tune your zither or give you some tips on crop rotation?"

Norment pointed out at the surrounding darkness. "Good-bye for now, gentlemen."

We said good-bye.

Four

Our meeting with Lew Marker had been postponed until 1:30 and shifted to the producer's vast offices in the Main Administration Building. When we entered the huge reception room, his pretty red-haired secretary exclaimed, "This is exciting!"

Groucho, dead cigar clenched in his teeth, went loping across the pale gray carpeting to her large, wide desk. "Yes, isn't it? I don't know about you, my dear, but my blood pressure just went up ten points. If it goes up another ten, I've half a mind to sell." Resting an elbow on her desk, he leaned in close. "What exactly are we excited about?"

"I meant I was excited. What with two big events here at the studio in the same day," she explained, reaching down to slide open a desk drawer. "That terrible murder, of course, and then my getting to meet you. I was elated when Mr. Marker told me to write your name in his appointment book. . . ." She paused, looking past him and in my direction. "And yours, too, Mr. Mumby."

"Denby," I corrected as I walked closer to the desk.

"Yes," she agreed. "Anyhow, Mr. Marx, I've been a fan of yours since I was so high and—"

"I've been high myself on a few occasions, but it never prompted me to like Groucho Marx," he confided.

She produced an autograph album from out of the open drawer. "I know this is gauche and adolescent, but . . . could you write something for me?"

With a bound, Groucho seated himself on the edge of her desk and crossed his legs. "I accept the challenge, my sweet. How's this strike you? 'Shall I compare thee to a summer's day? Thou art more lovely and more temperate: rough winds do—' "

"No, no," she interrupted, shoving the book toward him. "I meant write your name in my autograph book."

He accepted the book and dropped clear of the desk. "I offer this wench a sonnet, Rollo, and she says she'll settle for a cheesy autograph."

She looked perplexed for a few seconds, then smiled. "Oh, I see, you're being silly, Mr. Marx."

He slapped the book on the desktop and found a blank page. "I am, yes, I must confess," he admitted. "I have, alas, been suffering from silly spells ever since that fateful trip up the Orinoco. Naïve innocent that I was when I enlisted, I thought Orinoco was a vegetable and you can imagine my surprise and chagrin when I found myself coxswain on a leaky rowboat traversing the fish-infested waters of—"

The intercom atop the desk made a sudden squawking, throat-clearing sound and then a nasal voice inquired, "Has Groucho showed up yet, hon?"

"Yes, Mr. Marker. He just this minute walked in—with Mr. Wimpy."

"Denby."

"Time's a-wastin', kid. Show them in pronto."

30

"Right now, sir."

Groucho had finished scribbling in the book and he returned it to her, bowing. "I'll carry the memory of this chance meeting to my grave," he assured her. "But on the way back, somebody else is going to have to do the carrying. Farewell." He went slouching over to the door of the producer's office.

She was reading what he'd inscribed. "You put 'To Mitzi with the undying devotion of Groucho Marx,' " she called.

"Not as good, admittedly, as the summer's day stuff, but pithy and to the point, by Jove."

"The thing is, Mr. Marx, my name isn't Mitzi."

He shrugged one shoulder. "There's little or nothing I can do about that at this late date, I fear," he told her. "You might take the matter up with your parents. If they're out of town, we've had excellent results with the village blacksmith. You'll find him under the spreading chestnut tree most afternoons from one to five." He bowed again, opened the door, and backed into Marker's office.

She nodded at me. "I suppose he's like that most of the time, Mr. Dumphy?"

"Yep, he's even like that when I'm traveling under the name of Denby." Grinning at her, I followed in Groucho's wake.

I never liked that kraut," admitted Lew Marker. "All that artsy crap in his films, German Expressionist hooey. And he couldn't keep his hands to himself."

"Where'd he keep them?" Groucho was sitting deep down in a black leather armchair that faced the producer's desk.

Marker was a deeply tanned man, short, in his late forties.

31

He was wearing pearl gray slacks and a yacht club blazer with an intricate gold crest on the breast pocket. There were nine stovepipe hats scattered across the top of his Swedish Modern desk. "The last one Denker made a pass at fell for it," he said, scowling. "Poor kid, she'd dead."

Groucho asked, "Felix was romancing Marsha Tederow?"

"You heard about her getting killed in that auto accident a few days ago, huh?" He shook his head forlornly. "Real shame. She had a really terrific little ass. I could never get to first base with Marsha, but she sure went for that kraut."

"His wife knew about it?"

"The Valkyrie?" Marker started searching for something amid the array of upright black hats. "There isn't much that Erika doesn't know about what's going on here at Mammoth, Grouch. But I don't think she gave a good goddamn about his fooling around. Theirs wasn't exactly a love match and I don't even think they were living together anymore."

"So Erika wouldn't knock her husband off because she suffered a sudden fit of jealousy?"

The producer located a carved-ivory cigarette holder. He glanced up at Groucho, tapping the holder against his perfect front teeth. "You guys planning on playing detective again?"

"Not at all, Lew," he said, shaking his head. "Just curious, since we helped discover the body. Let's forget about murder altogether and chat about our brilliant *Cinderella on Wheels* scenario. I've been led to believe you're enamored of it."

"In a minute." He inserted a cigarette into the holder, picked up a lighter that was shaped like a miniature Oscar. After the cigarette was burning, Marker gestured at the spread of stovepipes with his free hand. "You two are experts on comedy."

"Frank is the expert on comedy," Groucho informed him. "My specialty is diseases of the knee."

"Seriously, Grouch, which of these hats strikes you as the funniest?"

Groucho sprang from his chair to scrutinize the collection. "None of them, Lew," he concluded. "Oh, maybe that scruffy one there next to the framed photo of those sideshow freaks is moderately amusing, but otherwise—"

"That's a picture of my wife and two kids."

"Ah, sorry. The bearded lady fooled me," said Groucho. "Based on nearly a century of experience on the legitimate stage, Lew, plus six months riding shotgun on the Deadwood Stage, I have to conclude that no hat is any funnier than the comedian who's wearing it."

"Look, they brought these over from a costume warehouse this morning," explained the producer. "Each one's a little different. What I want to know is, which type would look best on Robert Taylor?"

"Robert Taylor the revered clown, you mean?"

"Robert Taylor the matinee idol. It looks like I can borrow him from MGM for *Oh, Mr. Lincoln!*"

Eyebrows climbing, Groucho took two steps back. "You're contemplating producing a serious drama?"

"C'mon, Grouch, *Oh, Mr. Lincoln!* was a hit farce on Broadway for two years," said Marker, somewhat annoyed by this point. "F. Scott Fitzgerald turned in a swell script. And Ben Hecht is doing a terrific rewrite."

"Hecht would look amusing in that stovepipe next to your coffee mug."

"It's goddamned Robert Taylor who has to look funny as Abe Lincoln," he said. "I think the kid is on the brink of being a marvelous comic actor."

33

"All I know is that every time he bats those eyelashes of his, I snicker," conceded Groucho. "Now that we've made it through the headgear problem, can we chat about our sensational movie idea?"

The sun-brown producer took a deep drag on his cigarette holder, inhaling smoke and then slowly letting it out. He glanced over at me, saying, "That was a great radio show you guys had going, Denby. *Groucho Marx, Private Eye.* Funny as hell."

"Thanks," I said. "We think *Cinderella on Wheels* is even funnier and—"

"We're going to need a new title, fellows."

"Oh, so?" Groucho returned to his chair and slumped into it. "Why is that, Lew?"

"How does *Prince Charming on Wheels* strike you?"

"Why?"

"I really like the idea of inheriting a rinky-dink bus line," he told us. "Although I've been wondering if a railroad might be even funnier."

"It would not be, no. Why Prince Charming?" Groucho was sitting up straight, eyeing the producer.

"I've got a deal in the works with George Raft's people," he said. "He hasn't done much comedy so far, but I've got a feeling he—"

"The only things George Raft can play," said Groucho, "are gangsters, hoodlums, thugs, and, if he really tries, maybe a cigar store Indian. He's so stiff he makes John Brown's body look lively."

"I'm sorry you boys feel that way, Grouch." His tan face took on an expression of deep sorrow. "Because George is really anxious and eager to work with you. Turns out he was an enormous fan of your radio show and tuned in every single week until it was dumped off the air." He exhaled more smoke. "Why did *Groucho Marx, Private Eye* do a flopperoo? Lousy ratings, I heard."

"Actually," Groucho told him, "it was the FBI that shut us down. They discovered that we were sending coded messages to enemy zeppelins by way of the Mullens pudding commercials. The code involved the sequence in which we listed the five flavorful flavors of pudding. If we started off with strawberry, that meant—"

"So it was lousy ratings, huh?"

"Most nights, according to our researchers, only George Raft was tuned in," said Groucho. "And, on rare occasions, my son Arthur, but only on the evenings when he wasn't off playing tennis with the likes of Don Budge and Alice Marble. Or her brother Elgin."

I leaned forward in my chair. "We think *Cinderella on Wheels* plays best with a girl as the focal character," I said, as politely as I could. "The idea of a woman competing in a man's world is—"

"What do you guys think about riverboats?"

"As a means of transportation?" I asked.

"We have a terrific riverboat on the back lot. See, George could inherit that instead of the railroad. Then in order not to lose the business he has to run a race down the Mississippi or—"

"And we could call it *Prince Charming Up the Creek*," said Groucho, standing up. "Do you actually have Raft signed up?"

"Not yet," answered Marker.

"Are you prepared to make us an offer on our scenario?"

"Not yet, Groucho."

"What say we get together again when you actually have your star set? We can talk about butchering our brilliant concept at that juncture, Lew."

"I'm also thinking airmail planes." The producer rose up from behind his desk, making a diving airplane motion with his left hand. "George Raft inherits a rinky-dink airmail service in the Andes. Could be funny as hell."

"*Prince Charming Meets Amos and Andes* we can call it."

"Groucho, you're not going to get very far as a screenwriter unless you're willing to make a few little concessions."

"When you have George Raft in hand, let us know and we'll talk changes."

"Fine, Grouch. That's the attitude I like to see."

Groucho picked up the stovepipe hat nearest the edge of the desk, leaned, and plopped it atop Marker's bald head. "And that's the funniest hat of the bunch by far," he announced. "Or maybe it's simply the delightful way you model it."

Then we left.

Five

Groucho heard about the challenge late that same afternoon.

Back in August he'd started renting a new office on the Sunset Strip. He occupied part of the second floor of a white colonial building that looked like something David O. Selznick might be intending to use in *Gone With the Wind*. It was around the corner from a funeral parlor, next door to a cigar store, and across the street from a delicatessen.

"Talk about convenient locations, Rollo," Groucho had remarked right after signing the lease. "If only there was an ironmonger downstairs, this would be a veritable paradise. Actually I'd settle for a tinmonger or, in a pinch, even a plasticmonger. Anything we can plant out on the front lawn to scare away crows. I've noticed of late that flocks of cockatoos are also attacking the crops, but we don't want to frighten off those cute little decorative rascals, do we?"

As twilight started spilling down across the Hollywood hills and drifting onto the Strip that evening, Groucho, as he later told me, was scurrying across the boulevard clutching a white paper bag that contained a pastrami sandwich, two kosher dill pickles, a wedge of marbled halvah, and the revised third act of Mellman the waiter's tragic comedy, *The Rape of the Lox.* In an unguarded moment, Groucho had actually agreed to give his favorite waiter at Moonbaum's Delicatessen an honest opinion of his opus.

"I must alert you in advance, Ira, my beloved landsman, to the fact that I haven't had an honest opinion of anything since the day I arrived in Hollywood," he'd warned the gaunt Mellman before he departed. "And that was way back when I came out here to help Father Serra install the slot machines in his missions."

Groucho made it safely through the herds of speeding Rolls-Royces, Jaguars, and pastel convertibles that were roaring along the Strip. He was stepping with relief up onto the opposite curb when a very plump middle-aged woman in a flowered rayon dress, cloth coat, and fox fur piece stopped in her tracks to stare at him.

"It's you," she exclaimed, poking a fat finger in his direction.

"No matter what your daughter says, ma'am, I never touched a hair on her head," Groucho assured her, readjusting his grip on his deli bag. "Of course, I can't be as positive about certain other sections of the dear girl."

"I mean, you're Groucho Marx, aren't you?" She was reaching into her imitation leather handbag.

Frowning, Groucho looked down at his chest. "I hadn't given it all that much thought," he confided. "But now that you mention it, Olivia, I suppose I must be."

"My name isn't Olivia, Groucho. I'm Mrs. Peter Goodman." Locating her autograph album, she held it out to him.

"I'll call you Pete for short." Groucho, as though he were being offered a dead cat, accepted the book.

Mrs. Goodman laughed. "I'm a big fan of yours."

Groucho looked up from the page he was autographing. Then he took a step back, scrutinizing the plump woman from head to toe. "You are indeed," he agreed. "Meet me at UCLA tomorrow at dawn and we'll run two or three brisk laps around the track. We should be able to get you down to fighting trim in time for your next heavyweight bout."

The plump woman laughed again. "You know what I truly like about your sense of humor, Mr. Marx? It's so gentle and kindhearted," she informed him. "My husband says you strike him as a mean-minded so-and-so, but he's absolutely cockeyed. You're as gentle as a lamb and a real softy at heart."

"I'd tend to side with your hubby, ma'am." He returned her book and her fountain pen. Taking hold of her fox, he bent and gave it a smacking kiss on its plastic nose.

When the woman read what he'd written in her autograph album, she made a stunned gasping noise. But by that time Groucho was jogging up the wide wooden steps to his second floor office.

His secretary stopped typing on her Underwood when he came slouching into the office. "We have a problem, Groucho," she announced.

Nan Sommerville was a feisty, muscular lady in her late thirties. She'd been a circus acrobat and then a stuntwoman over at MGM. Groucho maintained that she'd often doubled for Wallace Beery, but Nan denied that. She was a terrific typist and a wiz at filing. Just about her only flaw was an unfortunate tendency to fall hopelessly in love with magicians. In the months she'd been in Groucho's employ, Nan had gone through unhappy romances with the Great Marvelo and the Amazing Zambini. Because of the nature of her troubled love life, I had to keep urging Groucho not to greet her continually with, "How's tricks?"

As twilight pressed against the windows, Groucho slumped to a stop in front of her desk in the small reception room. "How come you haven't turned on the lights, Nanette my flower?"

"Because I work for a parsimonious skinflint who is always kvetching about the high electricity bills," she replied, reaching over to click on her desk lamp.

"You must be referring to Mr. Hyde, my alter ego, child," he said as he perched on her desk edge. "I myself am the soul of generosity and was just now flinging bags of ducats to every pauper I could find. This being on the outskirts of Beverly Hills, there were very few paupers to be had, however. I almost persuaded a director from Monogram, who only earned twenty-seven thousand dollars so far this year, to take a handout, but he decided it would ruin his status in town. I hope you've noticed, my dear, that I refrained from saying anything about buying the evening paupers or calling attention to the fact that the word *ducats* sounds quite a lot like the word ducks."

"I thought Joe Penner had exclusive rights to all duck jokes. Don't you want to know about the problem I alluded to when you came schlepping in here, Groucho?"

As he opened the paper sack and thrust his hand inside, he grew thoughtful and considered her question. "I always like to look on the bright side and avoid problems whenever possible, which is why everybody on the plantation has taken to calling me Julius the Glad Girl. Except for kindly old Uncle Tom, who calls me—"

"You've been challenged to a duel," his secretary informed him.

The half of a pastrami sandwich that had been en route to his mouth stopped in midair. "Don't tell me Errol Flynn is jealous of me again."

"Nobody's talking about swords or pistols. This is a proposed duel of wits."

"I could say, 'That lets me out.' But, due chiefly to that anguished expression on your face, Nanook, I'll refrain." After taking a bite of his sandwich, he continued. "Can you provide some vital statistics? Such as who's challenging me?"

"That ham."

He gestured toward the darkening windows with the hand that wasn't holding the pastrami sandwich. "This is Hollywood, ham capital of the universe. Pray, be more specific."

"Miles Ravenshaw."

Groucho carefully smoothed out the paper bag, placed the half of a sandwich gently upon it, and then dropped free of the desk. "Ah, the ham of hams, the prototypical hambone," he said. "What sort of duel does that schlemiel have in mind?"

Picking up her open notebook, his husky secretary said, "So far this afternoon, Groucho, we've had telephone calls from Dan Bockman of the *Los Angeles Times*, Norm Lenzer of the *Herald-Examiner*, Gil Lumbard of the *Hollywood Citizen-News*, and somebody who might possibly be named Harlan Waffle of the *San Diego Union*. They are all extremely eager to talk with you."

"And I'm extremely distraught over the obvious silence on the part of the *Westwood Shopping News*."

Nan tapped her forefinger on the page. "As I understand it, Felix Denker was murdered out at the Mammoth lot and you and Frank found the corpse."

"We were cofinders."

"Be that as it may. At exactly three this afternoon, Miles Ravenshaw, who is starring as Sherlock Holmes in the movie Denker was directing, held a press conference at the studio," she continued. "Now, Bockman and Lumbard attended, but Lenzer is relying on a handout he got from a publicity gal at Mammoth. So their accounts don't exactly jibe. In Lenzer's version, Ravenshaw called you a pretentious fathead. But Bockman insists he labeled you a fatuous fathead."

"I think it sounds better in the alliterative version, don't you, Cousin Agnes?" He returned to his sandwich. "In fact, if Rita Hayworth stands me up again this evening, I may just spend my time in the sewing room embroidering "Groucho is a Fatuous Fathead" on a set of dish towels."

"Okay, this is pretty much what that hambone actor had to say: 'Felix Denker was not only a brilliant cinema director, he was one of my dearest friends. It is a source of great regret that he didn't live to finish directing me in the role of Sherlock Holmes in Mammoth's lavish production of *The Valley of Fear.* I intend to devote every waking hour, when I'm not in front of the cameras, to finding the solution to this horrible murder. I vow to track down the person responsible and to see that the vicious killer is prosecuted to the full extent of the law.' Of course, Groucho, I can't imitate that drawly British accent he affects."

"May we cut to the part where I'm maligned and challenged?"

She turned to the next page. "Bockman asked him about you, mentioning that you'd found the body and that you'd built up quite a reputation as a successful amateur sleuth. How'd Ravenshaw feel if you beat him to the solution? To which Rav-

42

enshaw answered, and I more or less quote, 'As most everyone knows, I come by my investigative skills legitimately. Before I entered into my highly successful career in films, I was a much-respected inspector with Scotland Yard in my native England.' Now, pay close attention, Groucho, here comes the good part. 'Unlike a certain low comedian who has bungled his way, with a combination of hubris and dumb luck, through some recent murder investigations in this benighted community, *I* happen to be a professional.' Then Lumbard asked him if he was worried about competition from you. 'I fully suspect, old man, that once that baggy pants mountebank learns that Miles Ravenshaw is on the case, he won't even dare to compete.'" She leaned back in her swivel chair, shutting the steno book.

Groucho retrieved his sandwich and took a few more thoughtful bites. "What really wounds, Nanette, is that baggy pants bit," he confessed. "It slights not only my tailor but my sweet young daughter Miriam, whom I require to do all the ironing and heavy lifting at our ménage."

"What the gents of the press are extremely curious about, Groucho, is whether you'll accept Ravenshaw's obvious challenge or just turn tail."

"Obviously, with a tail like mine I can't afford to—"

The phone on the secretary's desk rang. Nan picked up the handset. "Groucho Marx Enterprises," she said and then listened for a moment. Placing her palm over the mouthpiece, she said, "It's Johnny Whistler."

Groucho set down his sandwich again and took the phone. "Johnny, you may tell your millions of radio listeners that the code of the Marxes requires me to accept any and all challenges—even when they originate with the likes of Miles Ravenshaw," he said. "I intend to take up the gauntlet. That is,

I'll do that just as soon as my staff and I determine what in the heck a gauntlet is. I thought I had spotted one at a jumble sale over in Glendale, but, alas, it turned out to be a gravy boat. Later on, after the ladies have adjourned, I'll recite a breathless account of how I sailed a gravy boat around the Horn and discovered—how's that, Jonathan? Oh, yes, you want my *concise* answer. Very well, just say that I accept the challenge and that no-good faigeleh can take a flying schtup at the moon. And you may quote me, Johnny."

Six

Jane and I got the news about an hour later.

We'd taken a walk along the beach after dinner. A heavy rain started up when we were about a block from the Bayside Diner and we let go of each other's hand and started running for the narrow, bright-lit little restaurant.

"Oh, darn," she said as we crossed the threshold.

"What? Hurt yourself?"

"No, I just remembered I bought a bottle of champagne for our celebration and I forgot to serve it."

"We got sidetracked," I reminded her, walking over to the counter and pulling a few paper napkins out of a dispenser. "I'll drink some out of your slipper before we turn in."

"If you think I'm going to walk around in soggy slippers for the rest of the week, you've got another . . . Hi, Enery." She accepted a few of the napkins and wiped rain off her face.

Now that Enery McBride's movie career was on the upswing, he'd switched to the night shift at the diner so he'd be available for studio work daytimes.

He smiled at us from behind the counter, then inquired, "Well, what do you think?"

"About what?" I inquired as I crumpled up the napkins I'd used for towels.

"I've got to gain another twenty pounds. Do I look any heavier than when you saw me last?"

"We saw you three nights ago, Enery."

Jane settled onto a stool and looked at him with her head tilted slightly to the left. "Well, you are looking more cuddly," she decided. "So I suppose the new heft is starting to show."

There were only five other customers in the place. Two crew-cut teenage boys hunched over hamburgers at the far end of the counter, identical twin platinum blondes arguing about a play script in one of the booths, and an unemployed projectionist named Reisberson trying to outwit the pinball machine. The radio atop the icebox was turned low and tuned to an Andy Kirk band remote.

"Why the hell do they want you to be twenty pounds fatter to play Mr. Woo's chauffeur?" I climbed onto the stool next to my wife.

"This is a different role I'm up for—over at Mammoth," Enery confided, resting both palms on his side of the pale yellow counter. "I'm going to be the voodoo priest in *Curse of the Zombies.*"

"Who else is in it?" asked Jane.

"In this one I'm trying to turn Heather Angel into a zombie, but Regis Toomey saves her in the nick of time and shoots me."

"With a cast like that," said Jane, "you ought to get top billing."

He nodded. "Absolutely. Clarence Muse and I are going to flip a coin to see which of us gets his name above the title."

"We really thought you were great in *Mr. Woo Takes a Chance*, Enery. Did Frank mention that to you?"

"When I asked him if he'd seen the movie, Jane, he just blushed, stammered, and said he had to use the john," Enery told her, grinning. "When he came back he did tell me I was a credit to my race, though."

"As long as we're here," said Jane, putting her hand on mine, "we might as well have something. Cup of hot chocolate, Enery."

"Me, too."

Enery moved to the stove and got a pan of milk heating. "I read *Hollywood Molly* almost every day in the *Times*, Jane," he said, reaching for a tin of cocoa off a shelf. "It's funny."

"You're absolutely right," she agreed.

The radio said, "Time now for America's favorite Hollywood reporter—Johnny Whistler."

Enery mixed the cocoa into the hot milk, then turned the radio up. "Maybe he'll mention me tonight. You never know."

". . . Good evening to you and you and especially you," Whistler was saying in his breathless, high-pitched style. "I'll be giving you an inside report on the biggest news in the movie capital today—the brutal slaying of director Felix Denker. Ironically, he fled Hitler's Nazi Germany just three years ago to come to America. He found fame and fortune here, yes, but today—in a yawning soundstage Felix Denker found death. . . ."

Enery set our mugs of cocoa in front of us and asked me in a low voice, "You discovered his body, didn't you, Frank?"

"Sort of."

". . . I'll also be sharing with you what I just learned during an exclusive interview with fading comedian Groucho Marx, who discovered the bloody corpse of the Nazi-hating Denker. Earlier this afternoon Miles Ravenshaw, who is playing the immortal Sherlock Holmes in the movie that the murdered man was in the midst of directing, vowed that he would find the person who killed his beloved associate. Ravenshaw, a former Scotland Yard inspector, also challenged Groucho Marx to beat him to the solution. Although, as you know, Groucho has had some success solving a murder case or two here in Tinseltown, Ravenshaw asserts that luck and not skill was the reason for that. Groucho, you'll be happy to learn, assures me that he will find the killer of Felix Denker long before Ravenshaw. The Burbank police have no comment on this battle of the actors. We'll get back to these exciting stories and others right after Martin Terman brings you a word about Weber's Beautybar Bath Soap. . . .''

"I didn't know you guys were back in the detective business," said Enery, leaning an elbow on the counter.

"Neither did he," said Jane.

"Could be Groucho is going to work on this one solo." I picked up my cup and took a sip of the chocolate.

"C'mon, Frank, don't mope," said Jane, giving me an encouraging poke in the ribs. "You and Groucho are partners. Besides, if you want my opinion, he couldn't solve a mystery without your help."

I gave a halfhearted shrug. "We'll see. I suppose he—"

The door of the diner came flapping open and Groucho, clad in a yellow slicker and rain hat, came hurrying in out of the wet night. Removing his dead cigar from his mouth, he slouched over to us. "I had a suspicion you'd be hanging out in this seedy den," he said. "Gather as many of your belongings as you can load in a middle-sized Conestoga wagon and let's be up and doing. The game's afoot again, Rollo. In fact, by this time it's closer to a foot and a half and growing rapidly."

Our beach cottage on Mattilda Road in the town of Bayside had a large living room and that gave Groucho quite a bit of space for pacing.

I was sitting on our new sofa, yellow legal pad open on my knee, and Jane was perched, long legs crossed, on the arm of an armchair.

The night rain continued to fall enthusiastically, hitting hard on our slanted shingle roof and brushing at the windows.

"Okay, Watso," Groucho was asking, "are you absolutely certain you want to embark on another investigation?"

"I am, yeah."

"Keep in mind that it's my honor and not yours that's been besmirched by Ravenshaw," he said, pacing bent-legged over our pale tan carpet. "In a way I'm glad that happened, since it establishes the fact that I have any honor left. The point being, Rollo, that nobody's called *you* a fraud and a slipshod gumshoe."

"When they attack you, they attack me," I said. "At least when it comes to our careers as amateur investigators."

"Frank's going to help out on this one," Jane told him. "So let's get down to business."

Groucho halted, eyeing her. "You are an admirable young woman," he conceded. "I'm sorry now that I ever warned Franklin to avoid any young lady who had a brain larger that an avocado pit. You've turned out to be okay, sis."

"How about starting," she suggested, uncrossing her legs,

"with a list of possible motives for the killing of Felix Denker?"

"I was hoping we'd commence with a list of toys I wanted for Christmas," he said, returning to his pacing. "But I have to admit your suggestion is better. Don't forget, however, that an Erector set is my number one want. If it lives up to its name, I—"

"Motives," she repeated, leaving the arm of her chair and heading for the kitchen. "Coffee, Frank?"

"That'd be swell, Jane."

"All righty," said Groucho, watching her walk away, "why would anyone want to knock off Denker?"

"He was an arrogant shit that most everybody disliked," I offered.

Nodding as he strolled the carpeting, Groucho said, "That's one possibility, to be sure. A lot of people weren't fond of him. But a lot of people don't like me and I haven't been shot."

"Not yet," I said. "I don't actually think he was murdered because he was a pain in the ass to work with, but there still might be a work-related reason. And there are a lot of strange people in Hollywood."

"You think so, Ramona? I hadn't noticed," said Groucho. "I suppose it's possible that a disgruntled actor, writer, or studio hand got angry enough to lower the boom on Felix, but that strikes me as unlikely. We're looking for a more serious motive here."

Jane said, "Before you get off the topic of disgruntled colleagues, fellows—what about that drunken lady scriptwriter they unearthed in the vicinity?"

"Clair Rickson." I shrugged one shoulder. "We'll have to find out what the hell she was doing there, sure."

"I notice Johnny Whistler didn't mention her at all," she continued. "Think the police told him not to?"

"Might well have been the studio," said Groucho. "One more thing for young Franklin to investigate once a new day has dawned."

"I know Clair well enough to telephone her—provided Jack Norment hasn't locked her away as a material witness."

"Or a suspect," added Jane.

"Meantime, how about a domestic motive?" I suggested. "That'd make his wife, Erika Klein, a possible suspect."

"Lew Marker, prince of producers, told us Erika was too indifferent to her hubby to work up much in the way of jealousy or hatred."

"*He* says."

"We're definitely going to have to poke into the home life of Felix Denker, so jot that down on our list of flatfoot chores." Groucho slowed, dropped into the armchair Jane had vacated. "And we'll have to find out if he was fooling around with any young ladies besides Marsha Tederow. Make that find out who they were. There's bound to have been more than one, since Felix was what Carl Jung calls 'a dodgosted tomcat.'"

"That's a very good Jung impression," observed Jane, returning with three cups of coffee on a tray.

"Oy, what a night," complained Groucho. "First Johnny Whistler alludes to me as a failing comedian and now the mate of my boyhood chum razzes my mimic abilities."

"Whistler referred to you as *fading* not failing." Jane handed him a cup of coffee and then brought one over to me. "That isn't, the way I see it, quite as bad, Groucho."

"I suppose that's true, Nurse Jane."

Jane settled into our bentwood rocker, cup cradled in both hands. "What about the Nazi angle?"

"That was going to be my next recommendation," said

Groucho. "Denker was active in organizations like the Anti-Nazi League and he raised quite a bit of money for that and similar organizations. On top of which the Gestapo must've had his name on more than one shit list."

"If he had been in Berlin, I can see assassinating him for his opposition," I said. "But using a German agent to bump the guy off in this country is something else again."

"Make a note that we're going to have to find out just how important Felix was to his former countrymen." Groucho slid a cigar out of the pocket of his tweedy sports coat, unwrapped it, and put it in his mouth. He didn't bother to light it.

"Also how important Erika Klein is to the Nazis," I added. "Do they want her dead, too? Could be she's the real target and they were just warming up on Denker."

"I don't much care for the lady—if she were a little heftier, she could be playing a leading role in something by Wagner—but I'll go talk to her tomorrow."

"She may be grieving."

"All the grief she felt for Denker she probably got over about an hour or less after she heard the fellow was defunct."

"I know somebody in publicity out at Mammoth, a leftover from my *L.A. Times* days," I said, making another note in my legal tablet. "I'll see what background stuff I can dig up on both of them."

"Be helpful if we can get a look at the autopsy report, too," said Groucho, taking the dead cigar out of his mouth so he could drink some of his coffee. "Sergeant Norment seemed moderately cordial toward you, Rollo. Can you get a copy of that and maybe his report on the murder?"

Poking my tongue into my cheek, I considered the ceiling beams for a few silent seconds. "Jack Norment's not a bad guy, but I'm not sure how cooperative he's likely to be," I answered finally. "With Ravenshaw holding press conferences, Norment may think we're all doing this for the publicity."

"We are," reminded Groucho. "Be that as it may, I intend to do a thorough job—so see what you can pry out of him."

Jane rocked slowly in the chair. "It would be helpful to find out what Ravenshaw's up to. Do you think he's actually going to try a real investigation—or was that plain and simple baloney?"

"It's difficult to predict what a showboat like Ravenshaw is going to do. Any ideas, Frank?"

"I can also talk to my Mammoth publicity contact about Ravenshaw's plans. M. J. McLeod owes me a couple favors."

"Notice how he uses initials," Jane told Groucho. "That's so I won't realize he's talking about Mary Jane McLeod, with whom he once carried on a torrid romance."

"Tepid romance," I corrected. "Four years ago that was, long before you and I ever met. And the whole dull thing only lasted six and a half weeks."

"Notice that he doesn't mention that five of those six and a half weeks were spent in a motel in Caliente with the venetian blinds tight shut the whole darn time."

"Children, children," cautioned Groucho. "As someone who's always trod the straight and narrow path, especially when it passed anywhere near a house of ill repute, I don't like to hear references to salacious conduct on the part of my disciples." He drank just about all his coffee. "Now then, let's review what we've got on our list thus far." He held up his left hand, fingers spread wide, and ticked them off with his unlit cigar as he spoke. "Frank talks to the tempestuous M. J. McLewd—"

"That's McLeod, and don't believe a word Jane says."

"Frank learns from this blameless candidate for sainthood all he can about Felix Denker and his missus, Erika Klein," resumed Groucho. "He also worms news of Miles Ravenshaw's plans out of her. In his spare time, he contacts Sergeant Norment and acquires the Denker autopsy report and anything else he can slip under his coat. I need a good pencil sharpener, by the way. Meanwhile, I'll pay a condolence visit to the Widow Erika and find out what she thinks happened to her spouse. It also might not be a bad notion to drop in on Professor Ernst Hoffman for a wee chat."

"I met him once at your office," I said. "He's active in several anti-fascist organizations, isn't he?"

"That's Ernie, yes," said Groucho. "He also knew Denker and Erika in the Old Country—and he's kept in touch with them since they all came to America."

"He's the guy who teaches at Altadena Community College?"

"Yep, he's been in their German literature department ever since he got here from Berlin," said Groucho. "Ernie's specialty is Goethe. In fact, he and I have been meaning to write a philosophical cowboy yarn to be called *Goethe 'Long Little Dogie*. But, law me, we just can't ever seem to find the time."

"Groan," observed Jane.

"I could've added that we're also contemplating a Civil War epic to be known as *Faustus with the Mostest*. Be thankful I spared you that."

I leaned forward, picking up my cup. "We should find out what we can about Marsha Tederow, too."

"Who's she?" asked Jane.

"She was an assistant art director on *The Valley of Fear*,"

54

I explained. "She was killed in an automobile accident just a few days before Denker got shot."

"Two people connected with the same movie," said Jane. "That does sound a mite suspicious."

Groucho asked me, "Think you can get a look at the accident report?"

"Norment might help. If not, I can talk to somebody on the *L.A. Times.* I'll also see what they've got in the morgue files on Marsha Tederow's accident—and on her."

"Right, since we already know she was one of the lasses Denker was entangled with," said Groucho.

"You should also check and see how well Miles Ravenshaw knew her," suggested Jane.

"Right you are," said Groucho approvingly. "It might be we have nothing more than a nice simple love triangle here. Or, on the other hand, it might be that some Martians left over from Orson Welles's Halloween party invaded Mammoth and shot him. At his point, children, we don't actually know a damn thing."

"You know that you and Frank make a great team and you've cleared up a couple of tough murder cases over the past year," Jane said to him. "You're likely to do it again with this one. So don't look so hangdog."

"The reason I look so hangdog, my dear, is that they hanged my dog just before I drove over here. I warned him they wouldn't put up with cattle rustling in Beverly Hills, but he paid me no mind." He got to his feet, curtsied, and walked over to her. Bending, he kissed the top of her head. "I appreciate, though, your vote of confidence, as does every red-blooded Eagle Scout in this great land of ours. If I had any need to locate an eagle, I'd join the scouts myself. But for now, let me just state for the record—and the record we're alluding to is the Boswell Sisters' version of *"Flat Foot Floogie"*—let me state for the record, I say, that you deserve all the honors that this great state of ours has heaped upon you by naming you the Daughter of the Regiment, the Girl of the Golden West, and the Sweetheart of Sigma Chi. Although why Frank allows you to fool around with all those oafish fraternity boys is beyond me. It's also beyond Pasadena, and if we're going to reach there before daybreak, we've going to have to use those little electric prods on all the sled dogs." He kissed the top of her head once more before returning to his chair.

I started to set the legal pad aside, then stopped. "Four," I said.

"This is an odd time to be playing golf," observed Groucho.

"I just remembered the four Denker scribbled on that copy of *The Strand*."

"Ah, yes, the Clue of the Dying Message."

"A four? You didn't mention that either, Frank."

"May not mean a damn thing, but it looked like Denker dipped his finger in his own blood and started to write something on the cover of a magazine that was on the table next to the chair he died in."

"What sort of four?" She came over to sit close beside me on the sofa.

"Open-topped-style four." I drew it on the pad.

Frowning, Jane took my fountain pen from me. "This is a trick Rod Tommerlin taught me when I was working on *Hillbilly Willy* with him," she explained. "We did a sequence last year where some Nazi spies snuck into Weedville, Willy's hometown." She added three lines to the number four and converted it into a swastika. "It's a surefire and easy way to draw a perfect swastika."

"If we knew that Denker used a similar method to construct his Nazi insignias," said Groucho, who'd come over to the table to watch what Jane was doing, "we'd have something."

"What would we have?"

My wife said, "Maybe that he was trying to say that a Nazi had shot him."

"I don't know, Jane," I said slowly. "It's sure a possibility, I guess. But maybe the guy was only drawing a four—maybe, though I hope not, in his last moments his bloody hand twitched and scrawled something that vaguely resembles a four."

"Don't be so hangdog, Franklin," warned Groucho. "At this stage, we need every clue we can get and I think it's darned nice of your long-suffering missus to provide us with such a jolly handsome one." He stood up, stretched. "We're going to have to dig into the Nazi angle anyway and this gives us one more reason to do that."

I stood up, too. "It's nice being back in the detective business, Groucho," I told him.

"I haven't been this overjoyed, Rollo," he confided, "since I was runner-up in the Miss America contest back in 1926."

Seven

With a bundle of newspapers under my arm, I paused in the open doorway of Jane's studio. "Busy?" I inquired.

"Shouldn't you be shouting 'Wuxtry wuxtry'?" She set her pen on the taboret, capped the bottle of India ink, and smiled at me. "Find out anything new in those newspaper stories about the Felix Denker murder?"

I'd driven over to the outdoor newsstand on Bayside Boulevard earlier in the morning and picked up early editions of all the Los Angeles–area newspapers they had. After spending more than an hour going over them and taking notes, I left the sofa and went in to share my findings with my wife.

Jane was wearing a candy-stripe blouse and dark skirt and she had her auburn hair tied back with a twist of green ribbon. "Give me the important stuff first," she requested. "How many times did they mention you?"

"Hey, the *L.A. Times* also mentions you." I deposited my bundle atop a filing cabinet and located the *Times*. "Here it is. . . . 'Groucho Marx will be assisted by Frank Denby, a screenwriter who's married to popular cartoonist Jane Danner,

creator of the hit comic strip *Hollywood Molly* (see page 23).'
Actually, Jane, you got more space than I did."

"That's because they run my strip. But you did get promoted to screenwriter."

"It's only that screenwriter sounds better than unemployed radio writer."

Jane eyed me. "Maybe I shouldn't have taken down those No Sulking signs."

"What I miss more are the spittoons." I moved closer to her. "My guess about when Denker was killed was pretty close. The police estimate he died sometime between eight and ten Monday night."

"And the weapon?"

"A thirty-two Smith and Wesson revolver, which hasn't turned up so far." I glanced at the daily strip she'd been inking. "Looks great."

"Less flattery and more gory details," she requested, leaning and kissing me on the cheek.

I returned the kiss, then took a step back. "Okay, one of the stories mentions that Denker owned a thirty-two Smith and Wesson and that the police haven't been able to find it at his home or in his office at Mammoth."

"So he might've been shot with his own gun?"

"Might've, sure."

Jane asked, "And what, at long last, does your pal Sergeant Norment have to say about the mysterious Clair Rickson?"

"Not a damned thing."

"Nada?"

"Exactly—she isn't mentioned in any of the accounts," I told her. "I tried to phone Clair a few minutes ago and her answering service says she's sick and won't be returning any calls today."

"Think they've got her in the pokey?"

"I'll attempt to find out."

"Did Norment announce that they have *any* suspects?"

"All he's told the press is that they have several good leads that he's not ready to discuss," I answered. "Dan Bockman's story claims the cops are looking for an electrician who was fired from Mammoth a week back after a row with Denker on the set of *The Valley of Fear*. No name given, but this lad is supposedly a German who goes along with all Hitler's Aryan theories."

"Does that sound plausible to you?"

"Only if you can explain why Denker would let a guy who swore he'd get even for getting canned close enough to shoot him—and maybe with his own damn gun."

"There wasn't, you said, any sign of a fight—Denker didn't tussle with his killer. Try to stop him?"

"Nope, and the medical report confirms that."

"That could mean a friendly killer."

"Yeah, somebody he knew and probably even trusted."

"Where was his wife when he got shot?"

"That's in Norm Lenzer's story," I said, nodding back at my collection of newspapers. "Erika Klein left the Mammoth studios, checked out at the main gate, at a quarter after six that night. Didn't sign in again until nine-thirty the next morning."

"There goes the domestic motive."

"Unless she hired somebody to knock her husband off."

Jane said, " 'Hi, Felix, you don't know me, but I'm the thug your missus hired to shoot you. All in the family, as it were, so there's no reason to put up a struggle.' Nope, not very believable."

"Well, there are a lot of ways to get somebody to sit still

while you assassinate him," I said. "But it is sort of unlikely that it was a hired gunman."

"What does Norment say about the number four that Denker scrawled on the magazine cover?"

"Not a hell of a lot. According to Bockman's story, the Burbank police don't attach too much importance to the alleged dying message," I told her. "That, however, could just be a cover-up on Norment's part."

Jane pushed back from her drawing board, stretched by reaching both arms high. "Do they link Marsha Tederow with Denker?"

"Not yet, although a couple of stories talk about a possible Sherlock Holmes jinx. You know two people associated with the movie die violent deaths within a week." I crossed over to sit in her wicker armchair. "I dug up a few articles about her auto accident out of our pile of old newspapers in the washroom. Small back-page items."

"Marsha Tederow wasn't famous."

"Her Chevy coupe skidded on a rain-slick stretch of Mulholland Drive. Car went clean off the road and into a gully," I said. "It exploded, caught fire, and she was pretty badly burned."

"Hell of a way to die."

"Yeah," I agreed. "It didn't strike the police as anything but an accident. But maybe they'll look into it again because of the tie-in with Denker."

"You and Groucho got mentioned in most of the stories about Denker's murder?"

"Overlooking what really happened, all the stories credit him with discovering the body," I said. "And there are separate stories in most papers about the challenge." I selected a paper off my stack and turned to page three. " 'Groucho Marx Versus Sherlock Holmes' is the headline on this one. Others are variations. Even though they admit that Groucho and I have been successful at solving a few murder cases, they treat this whole business as sort of a joke. Maybe that's because Miles Ravenshaw is involved."

"I think you guys are a terrific team," said my wife, "but you have to admit that Groucho is a very difficult person to take seriously, Frank."

"Yeah, you're—"

The phone on her taboret rang. Jane answered, listened for a moment, wrinkled her nose, and handed me the phone. "Sergeant Norment himself."

"Morning, Jack," I said into the mouthpiece.

"It's come to my attention, Frank, that you've been trying to contact me."

"I imagine you've heard that Groucho Marx and I would like to look into the Denker murder," I began. "I was hoping I could get a copy of the autopsy report and maybe see the photos taken at—"

"You're no longer working for the *Los Angeles Times*, correct?"

"No, Jack, but this—"

"Even if you were still an accredited newspaperman, Frank, and not a glamorous screenwriter, I wouldn't be obliged to share confidential police information with you."

"You did, though, let me look at stuff like that when I—"

"And Groucho Marx is an actor who paints on a mustache and chases blondes in lowbrow movies, isn't he? That's the Groucho Marx you're in partnership with?"

"It's not the Groucho Marx who's the dean of the law school at USC, no. The thing is—"

"You are also the pair who got Sergeant Branner of the Bayside police sent up for murder, aren't you?"

"C'mon, Jack, he was crooked. You sure aren't, so why—"

"Thanks for the vote of confidence, Frank," he cut in, sounding as though he was smiling his joyless smile again. "I'm somewhat busy, but I did want to deliver a short lecture to you. I'd be obliged if you'd pass the gist of it on to Groucho Marx." He coughed. "I'm in charge of finding out who killed Felix Denker. I'm doing that because it's my job, not as a cheap stunt to promote a movie script or a second-rate detective film I'm starring in. Since I know you, Frank, I won't throw you or Groucho out of any place I run into you unless you get too much underfoot and in my way. I'll even give you a cordial hello if we chance to meet, but I sure as the devil am not going to cooperate with you or with Groucho Marx or with some half-baked actor who goes around saying 'Elementary, my dear Watson.' You want any information on the case, read the papers. Good-bye."

As I handed Jane the handset to be hung up, she said, "You did a lot more listening than talking."

"That's usually the way it is with sermons." I gave her a summary of what Sergeant Norment had conveyed to me. "You think maybe he's right? With the Peg McMorrow case we had some personal reasons for poking around—Groucho had known the girl and he was certain she didn't commit suicide. And with the Dr. Denninger mess we both believed that Frances London couldn't have murdered him. This time, though, there isn't any reason like those to get mixed up with the killing."

"You two have proven you're good at solving mysteries," she reminded me. "Somebody killed Denker and that somebody is still running loose. There's nothing wrong with tracking down a killer—even if you weren't a close pal of the victim."

"My civic duty, you mean?"

She nodded. "And besides, we can use the publicity."

While I was examining my conscience, Groucho was barging into his Sunset office with a paper bag from Moonbaum's tucked up under his arm like a football. "How's tricks?" he inquired, sliding to a stop in the vicinity of his secretary's desk.

Very politely, Nan thumbed her nose. "You'll be pleased to know that I just started dating a brand-new fellow," she announced. "And he's a swell guy, gentle and kind. Unlike certain gargoyles I've worked for."

Depositing his bag on a clear spot on the desktop, Groucho pressed his palm over his eyes. "No help from the audience, please," he requested. "I shall now proceed to part the veil of mystery and guess this admirable specimen's occupation. I see . . . rabbits, a top hat, a watermelon, a blonde being sawed in half. . . . No, wait. Scratch the watermelon." He lowered his hand, opened his eyes wide, and pointed at Nan. "He's a magician. Am I right, young lady?"

"Okay, all right, Groucho," she acknowledged. "I do seem to have an affinity for professional magicians. There isn't, after all, any harm in that."

"It's better than exclusively dating trunk murderers or scat singers, true," he acknowledged as he extracted a bagel spread with cream cheese from the bag. "What's this latest example call himself?"

"Zanzibar the Astounding."

Nodding, Groucho said, "I think Chico, Harpo, Zeppo, and

I worked with him back in vaudeville. Irving Zanzibar. About five two, two hundred and sixty pounds, a wart here, and a mole here. That him?"

"He happens to be suave and handsome, looks a lot like that actor Edmund Lowe."

"Nobody looks like Edmund Lowe," he informed her. "Not even Edmund Lowe. It takes two makeup men three hours to get Edmund Lowe to look like Edmund Lowe. Or possibly it takes three makeup men two hours." He sighed, took a bite of his bagel, sighed again. "And that ends our fun-filled visit with Miss Lonelyhearts for today, boys and girls. To business."

Nan picked up a manila folder and opened it. "I cut the reports on Felix Denker's killing from the newspapers. Then I typed up a precis of all the information."

"I'm touched, Nanook, for no one has ever given me a precis before. I was going to ask Santa for one, but the old duffer keep pushing me off his knee and whacking at me with his candy cane." Easing around to her side of the desk, he started sifting through the stuff in the folder.

"I also located Erika Klein," his secretary said. "She is, according to her, nearly collapsed with grief over her husband's death. But since you've been so supportive of causes that oppose Hitler, she's willing to grant you a brief audience. Eleven-thirty this morning. That okay?"

"Hunky-dory," he answered, nodding. "Where's young Widder Denker holed up at the moment? I heard she and Felix weren't cohabiting anymore."

"She's staying up in Bel Air, as a house guest at Merlinwood."

He set down the clippings he'd been scanning and raised his eyebrows. "The fabled eyrie of dashing silent swashbuckler

Guy Pope and the petite Alma Avon, known in my distant youth as 'America's Favorite Tomboy'?"

'That's the place, yeah."

"Supposedly Alma Avon hasn't set foot out of that castle of theirs since the day after *The Jazz Singer* opened. They were going to call her a recluse, but they decided she didn't get around enough to qualify for that." Frowning, working on his bagel, Groucho returned to his reading. "Why are they putting Erika up, I wonder?"

"She's actually living in one of their guest houses. The Popes have seven acres up there, remember?"

"I've never, alas, been a guest of the Popes or so much as set foot on the premises. He's been insanely envious of me ever since he saw a photograph of me in a pair of tights," explained Groucho. "And he may also have found out that if I hadn't put the arrow in the bow backwards during my screen test, I would've been the fellow who played Robin Hood in that classic silent film *The Rogue of Sherwood Forest.*"

"In 1924, when Pope starred in that movie, you and your disreputable brothers were doing *I'll Say She Is!* on Broadway."

"You're right, that long train ride from New York to Hollywood every day would've worn me to a frazzle. Just as well I didn't get the part," he conceded. "Although I did look awfully cute in that green Robin Hood suit. Green brings out the sparkle in my eyes and has been known to bring out the militia on occasion when—"

"Felix Denker's funeral and burial will take place Friday at ten A.M. It'll be at the Peaceable Woodlands Cemetery in Glendale," Nan told him. "You're invited, but not as a pallbearer."

"Just as well. You carry too many coffins and you get typecast. Look what happened to Benny Karloff."

"That's Boris Karloff."

"No, I was referring to Benny Karloff. He's Boris's cousin and went broke when the fad for pallbearer movies faded. Personally I thought the man was absolutely brilliant in *Carry Me Back to Old Virginny*. That's the one where he had to lug a coffin across several states single-handed to—"

"Judging from the news stories," Nan cut in, "the cops aren't any closer to solving Denker's murder than you are."

"They're hinting that a disgruntled studio electrician is a possible suspect." Groucho organized the clippings and notes back into a relatively neat stack and closed the folder. "In detective circles that's known officially as 'clutching at straws.' "

"May I give you a bit of advice, Groucho?"

He bowed, spreading his arms wide. "We're always open to constructive criticism here at the home office."

"Before you go up to Bel Air," suggested Nan, "you might want to wipe that blob of cream cheese off your chin."

Eight

The high stone walls around the Merlinwood estate were broken by a pair of wrought-iron gates. These were open wide, but a uniformed policeman was standing in the white gravel drive.

Groucho braked his Cadillac and rolled down his window as the cop came striding over.

"Can I help you, sir?" The officer was chunky and red-faced.

"I've got an appointment with Erika Klein. She's supposed to be living here at the moment."

"And you are?"

"Groucho Marx."

The cop leaned closer, studying his face. "Yeah, I suppose you must be."

"Believe me, Officer, if I had any choice in the matter, I'd be somebody else entirely," confided Groucho. "For a while I was going to be Father Flannagan of Boys Town, but then they decided my brogue wasn't up to snuff. On top of that, my snuff wasn't up to par. From there it went from bad to worse, with a side trip to Idaho."

"Uh-huh." The policeman pointed. "Park your car over there by the garages, then walk around behind and you'll see three cottages—cottages, hell, all of them are twice as big as my house in Pasadena. Anyway, Erika Klein is in the cottage on the far right."

"Who're you looking out for—Erika?"

The officer nodded. "Same people killed her husband may make a try for her. Nazi bastards. We've got her under an around-the-clock watch." Waving Groucho on, he stepped over to the side of the wide winding driveway.

There was about an acre of formal gardens, dotted with gnarled cypresses fronting the estate. Much of the foliage was faded, dry, touched with winter. The house itself was enormous, three stories high, built of gray stone and resembling the sort of castles Guy Pope had swashbuckled his way through during his heyday in the silents. You expected to see archers at the high, narrow windows, maybe a few lackeys up on the slated roof ready to send a cauldron of boiling oil splashing down on you.

As Groucho parked the Cadillac on the gravel, a dog started baying mournfully inside the twenty-five-room mansion. A large hound from the sound of him.

"I'll tell Baskerville you're looking for him," muttered Groucho, easing out of his car.

The day was still gray and overcast.

He rounded the garages and encountered a man clipping the tangles of ivy that climbed high on the gray wall of the imitation castle. He was tanned and in his middle fifties, and he attacked the ivy with an energetic grace.

"Good morning, Guy," said Groucho. "Excuse me for trespassing in your domain."

The actor stopped trimming, turned, and stared at him. "I know you, don't I?" he asked, looking somewhat perplexed.

"I'm Groucho Marx."

Pope smiled broadly. "Of course you are, yes," he said. "Forgive me for not recognizing you. My mind sometimes . . . Yes, Alma and I saw you and your brothers in *The Cocoanuts* on Broadway and you were hilarious. Nineteen twenty-eight, wasn't it?"

"Nineteen twenty-six."

"You were all marvelous fun, you especially—though somewhat too raucous for my Alma," said the actor. "I'd love to take you in and have you meet Alma again, but she's ailing."

"Sorry to hear that," he said. "But actually I'm here to visit with Erika Klein."

"A terrible tragedy, what happened to her poor husband. I never cared much for Felix Denker's films—much too pompous for my tastes—but I keep hearing the man was a genius." He shook his head sadly. "A dreadful thing that he was murdered on the set of his own movie."

"It was thoughtful of you to take in his widow."

Pope rubbed a forefinger across the bridge of his nose. "The least we could do," he said after a few seconds. "I wasn't actually the one who invited her, though."

"Oh, so?"

"No, it was . . ." The actor paused, frown lines deepening across his tanned forehead. "I'll think of it eventually, but I'm certain I wasn't the one. Not that we're not happy to lend a hand."

"Your wife maybe?"

"Wasn't my Alma, no. She's not strong enough to issue invitations these days."

"I must be going," said Groucho.

"Certainly pleasant running into you like this, Groucho," said Pope, smiling again. "We haven't seen each other for quite some time, have we?"

"If not longer."

After trotting along a red flagstone path and through a wooded area, you came to a clearing that contained three extremely rustic thatch-roofed cottages in a mossy glade.

"The seven dwarfs don't seem to be at home this morning," he said to himself, heading for the quaint house on the right.

The oaken front door creaked open and a tall, wide man stepped out into the gray late morning. He wore a navy blue double-breasted suit, his head was shaved to a glistening smoothness, and he had a Luger dangling from his right hand. "Stop right there, if you would, sir," he requested, pointing the gun at Groucho.

Things didn't go very smoothly for me at the Mammoth studios.

The main problem was that they wouldn't allow me to set foot on the lot.

When I rolled up to the gates at a few minutes shy of eleven that morning, a uniformed guard came over to my Ford. It wasn't Oscar from the day before. "Do you have business here, sir?"

"Yeah, I'm supposed to see M. J. McLeod."

The long, skinny guard, who appeared to be wearing the uniform of a somewhat shorter and fatter colleague, asked me, "What was your name, sir?"

"Was and is Frank Denby."

Nodding briefly, he returned to his guard shack. He had a slight limp in his left leg.

When my car radio started playing "Jeepers Creepers," I clicked it off.

The guard returned with a clipboard. "Frank Denby, you said?"

"That's right, yeah. Eleven o'clock appointment with M. J. McLeod."

He brought his clipboard up close to his face, studying the list of names attached to it. "Oaky doaks, here it is," he said eventually.

"Fine."

"The reason I didn't spot it right off, sir, is that it's been crossed out."

"How's that?"

"Your appointment has been canceled, Mr. Denby."

"Why'd that happen?" I'd phoned Mary Jane McLeod at her home the night before to set this up.

"Well, if I'm interpreting these little scribbles in the margin correctly, Mr. Denby, the order to cancel came from the chief of security himself," he explained, tapping the page with his forefinger. "Oh, and it also says you're to be denied access to the studio until further notice. I wasn't on duty when this came down this morning, so I wasn't aware—"

"Can I use your telephone to call Miss McLeod?"

"No, I don't think so, sir." He gave me a negative shake of his head along with a sympathetic smile. "You've apparently gotten yourself on somebody important's shit list, sir, if you don't mind my saying so. *No access* means no access at all. I wouldn't even risk taking the lady a note."

"Ravenshaw," I muttered.

73

"How's that, sir?"

"Just an old Armenian curse," I told him, and backed out into the gray late morning street.

The nearest public phone was in a bar down the block from the Mammoth spread. The place was called the Hawaiian Hideaway and when I stepped into its whiskey-scented dimness, the jukebox was playing a selection by Harry Owens and His Royal Hawaiians.

Hearing steel guitar music and tropical drumbeats at that hour, especially after you've been given the heave-ho by a motion picture studio that was supposedly considering buying a comedy of yours, is not a cheering experience.

Three bit players dressed as pearl smugglers were drinking Regal Pale beers at the warped bar and a seriously fat woman in her fifties sat alone at the only occupied table telling her own fortune with a bedraggled deck of tarot cards.

I hunched into the phone booth, which smelled strongly of recent illness, half shut the door, dropped in my nickel, and dialed the Mammoth number.

"Mammoth Pictures. How may we help you?" inquired a young woman through her nose.

"Publicity Department, please."

A moment later a girl with the voice of a failed actress answered, "Publicity. How may I help you?"

"M. J. McLeod, please."

I sensed a slight flinch and her next question showed a trace of wariness. "Who's calling?"

Deepening my voice some, I told her, "Richard Harding Davis of the *Denver Post.*"

"Please hold on, Mr. Davis."

"Hello?" came Mary Jane's uneasy voice.

"This is Richard Harding Davis, little lady. I'm hoping you remember the golden days we spent together side by side at the *Los Angeles Times*. My own memories are evergreen and—"

"Frank?" She lowered her voice to a near whisper.

"Hey, Mary Jane, why the hell am I barred from the—"

"Why do you think? Miles Ravenshaw went to Lew Number One right after his stupid press conference yesterday and told him it would be a nifty idea if you, Groucho, and any of your next of kin were kept out of here until after Ravenshaw cleared up the mystery of Felix Denker's murder."

"Looks like I'm doomed for all eternity, then, because that half-wit will never—"

"I didn't find out about Lew Goldstein's ultimatum about you until a few minutes ago, Frank. Too late to head you off."

"Will you suffer if you meet me off campus?"

It took her close to a full minute to think about that. "Okay, there's a little Mexican joint over on Nolan Drive, about six blocks south of us," she told me in a low, cautious voice. "Nobody from the studio ever eats there because the food is so dreadful. It'll be a safe place for us to meet. Twelve?"

"Shall we work out a series of passwords?"

"Still an idiot," she said, and hung up.

Nine

Groucho said to the man with the Luger, "Have you by any chance seen a motion picture entitled *Room Service*?"

"Never heard of it," answered the hairless man, somewhat perplexed.

"That's a relief, since it lessens my chances of being shot down like a dog. Of course, if I were going to be shot down like a dog, I think I'd prefer to be shot like a Saint Bernard. That way we can all have a snifter of brandy afterwards and—"

"Ah, you must be Groucho Marx." He slipped the gun away in his shoulder holster. "Miss Erika is expecting you, but I didn't immediately recognize you. You don't look like Groucho Marx."

"Why thank you, that's the nicest thing anybody's ever said to me." He approached the cottage doorway.

"Groucho, I'm terribly sorry." A slim, sternly pretty blond woman in her early forties appeared next to the large, wide man. She was wearing dark blue bell-bottom slacks and a black cashmere sweater. "Gunther can be overzealous at times. But considering that my husband was brutally murdered, I don't blame him for being cautious and protective."

"You think whoever killed Felix is also planning to kill you?"

"They've already threatened her," said Gunther.

"Oh, so?"

Erika smiled sadly. "Come inside, Groucho, and we can talk," she invited. "I'm afraid it can't be a long visit, since I'm far from over the shock of Felix's death." She retreated into the shadowy parlor.

Gunther stepped aside and nodded at the doorway.

The parlor was gloomy, the drapes drawn, the only light coming from a parchment-shaded floor lamp. The furniture was heavy and from the Victorian era. On the walls hung several large gilt-framed oil paintings of Alma Avon in some of her most famous movies, including *Tomboy, Little Nell,* and *Granny's Girl.* There were several large vases holding bunches of brittle dried flowers.

"Cheery." Groucho walked over to the empty fireplace and held out his palms toward it.

"It is somewhat somber," Erika acknowledged, settling into a purple Morris chair. "Right now, however, it suits my mood."

"How long have you been staying here?" Groucho sat in a claw-footed armchair facing the slim widow.

"Coffee, Miss Erika?" inquired Gunther from the doorway.

"That would be nice, yes," she told him, smiling. "Gunther and I have been here at Merlinwood for close to three months, Groucho."

"Oh, I had the impression, chatting with Guy Pope just now, that you'd only moved in very recently."

"I sometimes suspect that Guy, bless him, jumped off one too many balconies during his heyday," Erika said, touching at her temple, "and jiggled his brain. He seems to be getting increasingly forgetful."

"So who was it who invited you to live in this cottage?"

"Actually I'm a tenant, Groucho, but it was Guy and Alma who suggested the arrangement," she answered. "Felix and I became acquainted with them soon after we arrived here from Germany. Guy was inordinately fond of my late husband's *Ride of the Valkyries*. That was made in Berlin in 1929."

"And you and Felix separated because—"

"We simply decided it would be better to live apart for a time," Erika told him. "We remained devoted to each other, however. You must know that in the best of marriages, there are periods when you want to be away from each other."

"My wives tend to want extremely long periods of separation, followed by substantial alimony," said Groucho, taking out a new cigar.

"I'd appreciate it if you didn't smoke, Groucho."

"Sorry." He put the cigar away. "Who exactly is Gunther?"

"A very loyal fellow. He was Felix's valet in Berlin and emigrated to the United States with us," she explained. "When I moved to Merlinwood, Felix insisted that Gunther come along to look after me. As you've witnessed, Gunther is terribly devoted to me."

"Gunther mentioned threats to you."

Erika left her chair to cross to the mantelpiece. "These are photostats of the originals," she said, picking up two sheets of paper. "I turned the originals over to Sergeant . . . Norman, isn't it?"

"Norment." Groucho accepted the stats.

"I've made several copies. You can keep these for your files."

Both notes were hand-lettered in neat block capitals. The first said, "FELIX DENKER: THEY FAILED TO GET YOU IN GERMANY.

79

WE'LL SUCCEED." The other read, "ERIKA KLEIN. YOU'RE AS BAD AS YOUR JEW HUSBAND. YOU WON'T LIVE LONG."

"When were these sent?"

"Felix showed me his letter about a week ago," she said. "He wasn't as upset as I was. I persuaded him to give it to me, but unfortunately I hesitated about showing it to the police."

"You got this other one after Felix's death?"

"Yes, although I didn't know it at the time. The letter was in the mailbox here when I got home from the studio Monday night," Erika said. "I left Mammoth about six-thirty that night. If I'd stayed longer, I might have been able to—"

"Or you might've gotten shot, too. What about the envelopes these came in?"

"They weren't mailed, so there weren't any postmarks. And Sergeant Norment told me there were no fingerprints besides mine and Felix's on either note."

"Any idea who sent these?" He folded the letters and stuffed them away in an inside pocket of his sports coat.

"Yes, I do. I believe it was Franz Henkel, the studio electrician Felix had fired," she said, returning to her chair. "He'd made other threats to my husband, using similar language."

"How'd he do that, face-to-face or—"

"On the telephone, on two separate occasions. Felix told me that a man who sounded very much like that fascist had made some nasty anti-Semitic remarks and warned him that he wasn't going to be alive much longer."

Gunther entered carrying a dark wood tray that held two delicate cups, a small bowl of sugar cubes, and a carafe of coffee. "Anything else, Miss Erika?"

"Not at the moment. Thank you."

After plopping two lumps of sugar into his coffee, Groucho asked, "Suppose Henkel didn't do it—who else might want to kill your husband?"

"There are, which you know, quite a few groups right here in Southern California that support Hitler," she said, picking up her cup. "Everything from the German American Bund to those America First fools."

"But so far *they* haven't murdered anybody."

"So far they haven't been *caught* murdering anybody," said Erika. "I'm also certain that there are Nazi agents here, too, spies, saboteurs. Felix had been extremely outspoken in his attacks on the Third Reich."

Groucho drank some of his coffee, then set the cup on the table and stood. "I must be going," he announced. "I appreciate your talking to me."

Erika stood. "I've read about the murder cases you and your writer friend helped to solve," she said. "I'm hoping you'll be able to find out who killed my husband, whether it was Henkel or somebody else. Frankly, Groucho, I don't have much faith in the police. Although that may be because of our experiences with the police in Germany."

As she escorted him to the front door, Groucho said, "I'll try to keep you informed."

"You'll be attending the funeral on Friday, won't you?"

"Quite probably."

"Then we'll talk again there, if not before."

There was no sign of Guy Pope as Groucho walked back to where he'd left his Cadillac. Before he started the engine, he took out his cigar again and lit it. "Sometimes in Hollywood," he said to himself, "it's extremely tough to tell a performance from the real thing. I wonder if Erika really gives a damn about who killed Felix.''

He sighed out smoke, started the car, and drove away from Merlinwood.

Ten

You don't need a restaurant guide to tell you that a Mexican café owned and operated by a former Swedish character actor is probably not going to serve authentic cuisine. The smells of burnt pots and aging lard that gave the Señorita Rio Mexican Café its distinctive fragrance provided another reason why I'd ignored the mimeographed menu and ordered only a Dos Equis beer while I was waiting for Mary Jane to sneak over from Mammoth.

Olaf Hamsun, who'd played his last movie role in 1931, was sitting by himself at a small table near the door of his establishment, reading a two-day-old copy of *Film Daily* and, very dejectedly, eating a bowl of warm milk laced with oyster crackers.

There was nobody else in the little place, and I felt that if I sat here another ten minutes or so, I'd probably order some food just out of sympathy. I was speculating on what would be less god-awful, enchiladas à la Olaf or Swedish tamales, when M. J. McLeod showed up.

She entered sort of sideways, looking furtive, the way movie spies looked when keeping rendezvous in dark alleys. "Hello,

Olaf," she said as she passed his table. "How're you doing?"

"Business is picking up, Mary Jane. Two customers already and it's barely noon." He looked up at her hopefully. "How about a nice bowl of Stockholm chili?"

"Only a cup of coffee, thanks." She sat down opposite me. "I'll leave a huge tip. I always feel so guilty when I come here and don't eat."

"So why do you come here, then?"

"Because, dodo, it's a great place for clandestine meetings." Mary Jane was about my age, tall and dark-haired. She was talking in a low, confidential voice and I had to lean toward her to catch what she was saying.

"I didn't know Miles Ravenshaw had so much influence with your studio."

"With Randy Grothkopf backing him, he sure does."

"Your boss—the head of the Mammoth Publicity Department?"

"Him, right." She let out a forlorn sigh. "Because of the murder, *The Valley of Fear* is getting a hell of a play in the papers and on radio. Ravenshaw convinced Randy that his pretending to find out who bumped off Felix will get us even more publicity. That would be screwed up if you and Groucho actually did nab the killer. So you guys are barred from the lot. What's this floating in my coffee, Olaf?"

The owner had just placed a coffee cup in front of her. Squatting, he squinted into the cup. "How do you suppose a Mexican jumping bean got into your coffee?"

"We can assume," she said, "the darn thing jumped in."

Olaf picked up her spoon and was attempting to rescue the floating bean.

I suggested, "Suppose you just bring a fresh cup of coffee?"

"I'd have to charge another nickel for that."

"That's okay. Put it on my tab."

The unemployed actor straightened up and took the coffee away.

"Olaf was very funny in the movies," Mary Jane said, watching him shuffle toward his small, dismal kitchen. "That was, unfortunately, some years ago."

"Does anybody at Mammoth really believe that Ravenshaw is going to beat the police and Groucho and me to a solution?"

"Randy has pretty much convinced Lew Number One that a onetime Scotland Yard inspector ought to be smarter than a Burbank cop," she answered. "Goldstein was already sure that Ravenshaw was smarter than you and Groucho."

I took a sip of my warm beer. "Has that hambone actually done anything thus far?"

"He examined the scene of the murder at the Two-twenty-one-B set, using his Sherlock Holmes magnifying glass and accompanied by photographers from the *L.A. Times*, the Hearst papers, *Photoplay*, and *Motion Picture*," she answered, eyeing the fresh cup of coffee Hamsun had just delivered. She picked up her spoon, poking it into the coffee. "Olaf, there's something in this one, too. Down around the bottom of the damn cup."

"It might be another jumping bean, Mary Jane. One that drowned in the coffee pot."

She dropped the spoon next to the cup and pointed across at my bottle of beer. "Forget coffee, bring me one of those."

"Your friend got the last one I had in stock," he said apologetically, looking down at his scuffed shoes. "But I've got two Lucky lagers and a Regal Pale left."

Mary Jane assumed the expression of a small child who's just been abandoned in the deep woods by a wicked stepmother. "Lucky Lager," she decided after a few seconds.

Resting an elbow on the tabletop, I asked her, "What about Sergeant Norment and his crew? You can't lock them out of the studio. What's he come up with?"

"Jack Norment doesn't confide in me, Frank," she said. "But the scuttlebutt is he favors the notion that Franz Henkel may've killed Felix."

I straightened up. "That's the electrician he had fired?"

"Him, yes. Seems Henkel got in a couple of serious brawls during the three months he worked for us, proving he has a violent temper," Mary Jane told me. "He also tried to hand out some anti-Semitic pamphlets and, most important to Norment, he allegedly threatened to get even with Felix Denker."

"Get even how? By sneaking by the security people, breaking into the soundstage, and shooting the poor guy?"

"He didn't draw up an agenda and hand out copies, Frank," she said. "The quote I heard, third or fourth hand, was something like, 'I'll fix that dirty Jew for what he did to me.' "

"Did he also click his heels and shout, 'Heil Hitler'?"

"Most times murder in real life isn't like murder in the movies," she reminded me. "In the everyday world some goon will say, 'I'm going to kill that bastard one of these days,' and then actually go out and kill him. That's how the police catch most of their murderers, I'd imagine."

"Maybe, but Franz Henkel is too obvious a candidate."

"That's because you're thinking like a writer."

"What's Henkel say for himself?"

She paused to touch the side of the beer bottle Olaf had placed before her. "This feels awfully warm."

"I can bring you a glass full of ice cubes to pour it in."

"Never mind, no." She issued another sigh. "Franz Henkel

has apparently disappeared, Frank. He lived in a rooming house over in Manhattan Beach, but he hasn't been seen since the murder. You have to admit that's suspicious."

"Yeah, we better round up a posse and lynch him."

She shrugged. "Well, I think Ravenshaw is inclined in that direction, too." After tapping the Lucky lager bottle with the tip of her finger a few times, she pushed the beer aside and picked up her cup of coffee.

"Considerable silence seems to have descended on Clair Rickson," I said. "What do you know about her?"

A pained expression touched her face as she turned away from me to gaze at a faded bullfight poster taped to the splotched pale orange wall. "I was hoping, Frank, we could skirt this entirely."

"Skirt what? Is she involved in the murder somehow?"

Mary Jane sighed out a breath. "No, Clair is . . . well, she's just Clair." Turning to face me, she leaned forward and lowered her voice even further. "She apparently had some kind of violent quarrel with one of her boyfriends in the Writers Department Monday afternoon. That prompted her to go on one of her protracted solitary drinking binges in her office. Sometime in the middle of the night, she started wandering around the lot and, probably because she wrote the screenplay, she ended up on one of the indoor *Valley of Fear* sets. She'd brought a bottle with her and she sat down in the pub to finish it. She passed out and didn't wake up until the cops found her in the morning."

"Jesus, that's so unlikely it wouldn't even get by in *The Case of the Crucified Crooner.*"

"True nonetheless, Frank," she insisted. "Clair didn't get to the soundstage until long after Denker was killed. She didn't hear or see a damn thing. To help her get herself back on track and avoid a lot of embarrassing, notoriety, everybody's agreed to play down her involvement in this whole mess."

"Yeah, what I like about movie people is their altruism."

"Hey, lay off, buster. I'm leveling with you."

"Where's Clair?"

"Drying out at a private clinic."

"Which?"

She shook her head. "Randy might know. I don't," she said. "So help me."

I changed topics. "You knew Denker and—"

"Not well."

"Better than I did, since I never met him," I said. "If this missing electrician didn't kill him, who would you—"

"Since I'm not in a contest to solve this murder, Frank, I haven't given much thought to who done it."

I pushed my bottle of beer aside. "Okay, how about Marsha Tederow—did you know her?"

She nodded sadly. "We weren't close friends, but I had lunch with Marsha a few times and I liked her," she replied. "After she started her affair with Denker, she complained to me about him once or twice. My advice was to stay away from a son of a bitch who'd treat you like that, but she didn't follow it."

"How did he treat her? Physical violence or what?"

"He could be violent at times and I know he hit her more than once," she answered, trying her coffee and then wincing. "Why she kept meeting him at that damned love nest he set up, I don't know. Some weekends she spent just about—"

"Whoa, halt, Mary Jane. What love nest?"

She said, "Marsha lived in a small place up in Beverly Glen, which she shared with a roommate. Denker would meet her there sometimes, but that was only when the roomie was else-where." Mary Jane tried the coffee again, then set the cup down and slid it over toward the beer bottle. "Even though Denker wasn't living with his wife in recent months, he didn't want Marsha coming to his mansion. Probably so Erika Klein wouldn't be able to find out what he was up to. Anyway, he rented a beach house down around Malibu someplace. That's where they were meeting most of the time."

"Are the police aware of that hideaway?"

"I'm not sure," she said.

"Know specifically where the house is?"

"I don't have an address, no," she answered. "But a month or so ago, when I had to keep in touch with Marsha over a weekend because of a studio problem, she gave me the phone number."

"Do you still have it?"

Reaching down, she retrieved her large straw purse from the dusty floor. "I'm pretty sure I wrote it down," she said, poking her hand into the bag. She produced a very fat address book and started leafing through its pages. "Here's the number of a cowboy actor who was going to leave his wife and marry me but never got around to it. Here's a stuntman who was going to leave me and go back to his wife and never got around to that. Good, here's Marsha Tederow's number." She scrib-bled the telephone number on a paper napkin and passed it across to me.

"I can probably use a reverse directory and get the location of the place." I folded the napkin and put it in the breast pocket of my coat. "Now what about Erika Klein?"

Mary Jane produced a razzberry sound while making a

thumbs-down gesture. "A very cold, nasty lady," she said. "But, so I hear, a damned good historian. They all appreciate her at Mammoth, I know."

"From what I've learned so far about her and her husband, she wouldn't have been jealous about his affairs."

"No, they weren't the Nelson Eddy and Jeanette MacDonald of German refugees," she said. "I think he tried to keep his romantic interludes quiet because he was afraid she might get lawyers after him and sue for divorce. But, nope, Erika wouldn't shoot him down for jumping in the sack with poor Marsha."

"How about some dessert?" Olaf inquired as he approached our table.

"No," we answered simultaneously.

Eleven

Just beyond the palm trees and the stone deities in the court-yard of the Egyptian Theater on Hollywood Boulevard, he later told me, Groucho encountered a tall, lanky Santa Claus standing beside a copper kettle and rather halfheartedly clanging a small brass bell. "Give to the Community Charities Fund," the Saint Nick recited. "Help the less fortunate at Christmas."

Slowing, Groucho came to a stop, leaned, and peered into the kettle. There was what looked to be about twenty-five bucks in change and a few crumpled dollar bills within. "I'm less fortunate than just about anybody," he explained, dipping his right hand down toward the sprawl of money. "How much am I allowed to scoop up, my good man?"

Frowning, giving a negative shake of his head, he said, "No, no, the idea is to *give* us something."

"What kind of charity is that? When I have to give *you* something?" Groucho stepped back, scowling. "You look to be in much better shape than I am, which isn't saying much."

"You're being obtuse about how charity is supposed to . . ." The sidewalk Santa stopped, started laughing. "Oh, it's you, Mr. Marx. I didn't catch on right away that you were joking."

"Far too many people have been suffering from that problem of late," he confessed. "Whole vast audiences of people seeing *Room Service* for the first time claim to have had such experiences. A prominent New York motion picture critic dubbed the movie the greatest tragedy he'd even seen and three state troopers in Wisconsin voted me the greatest tragedian since Jean Hersholt."

"I guess you don't know who I am, Mr. Marx, but—"

"You mean you aren't Santa Claus?"

The man smiled through his whiskers. "I'm Leonard Hershberger," he said. "I had bit parts in *A Night at the Opera* and *A Day at the Races.*"

"What a coincidence. I had bit parts in those same movies," Groucho told him. "Two itinerant musicians claiming a distant kinship with me upstaged me throughout both those MGM epics."

"Actually, I thought you were terrific in both of those and you were very funny in *Room Service.*"

Groucho pressed a warning finger to his lips. "Don't go around saying anything like that too loudly," he cautioned. "They're liable to drop a net over you and haul you away. I haven't checked my Blackstone recently, but I think such remarks also violate the California sedition laws. I did check my Gladstone the other day, however, and if I can only remember what bus depot it's in, I'll be able to go to that slumber party after all." He located a four-bit piece in the pocket of his sports coat and tossed it into the pot. "Keep the change. And good luck, Leonard."

"Thanks, I'm optimistic," the unemployed actor assured him. "Things are sure to get better after the first of the year."

"If that giant meteor that's scheduled to flatten Los Angeles early next month swerves off course at the last moment, yes, life is going to be a bowl of cherries. And, frankly, I can't think of anything that sounds messier." He added some lint from his pocket to the kettle and hurried on his way.

When he reached Los Palmas, he crossed the street and hurried along toward Musso & Frank's Grill.

As he was going through the arched entryway and reaching out to push open the glass-paneled door, a passing tourist exclaimed to her companion, "That's Groucho Marx!"

Stopping, Groucho pivoted and pointed an accusing finger at them. "Have a care as to what you call an innocent bystander, my good woman," he warned. "Accusing someone of being Groucho Marx in this man's town is tantamount to slander. And calling him Bob Hope is tantamount to Paramount. Keep that in mind—and you might also keep the multiplication tables in mind, since you never know when you'll be called upon to multiply."

Curtsying, he backed on in to the restaurant.

"Oof," gasped the head waiter he bumped into.

"Good afternoon, Orlando," said Groucho after turning around and recognizing the plump man in the tux. "Am I too late for the free lunch?"

"Table for one, Mr. Marx?"

"Alas, I fear so, Orlando. All my family and friends have deserted me," he confided. "In fact, not five minutes ago, three total strangers deserted me."

Bowing very slightly and turning, the waiter invited. "Follow me, please."

As he was making his way along a row of booths in the beam-ceilinged main room, Groucho spotted Rosalind Russell, Merle Oberon, and Joan Crawford lunching together. "Top of the afternoon, ladies," he mentioned in passing.

Rosalind Russell smiled, Merle Oberon smiled, and Joan Crawford gave him the finger.

"She never forgave me for what happened in that phone booth in Tijuana," Groucho told the plump waiter, sighing at the distant memory.

About two minutes after he was settled in his booth and studying the menu, someone appeared beside his table.

"Jove, what a lovely treat for us all. It's the great detective himself."

Groucho glanced up to behold Miles Ravenshaw smiling down on him.

The Santa Claus I encountered was a short and chubby one and might possibly have been a woman under the red suit and fluffy white whiskers. This Saint Nicholas was sitting in a canvas director's chair on a grass sidewalk border out near the end of Sunset. Next to him leaned a large hand-lettered sign offering *MAPS of the STARS' Homes—Only 25 Cents!* A slight drizzle had commenced about ten minutes earlier and Santa was waving his handful of maps from under a wide polka-dot umbrella.

When I stopped at the stoplight next to the map vendor, he called out, "Hey, asshole! It's Christmas—buy a goddamned map!"

"Humbug," I replied, not bothering to roll down my window.

At the Coast Highway, I made a right turn. Using the reverse telephone directory that I kept in a drawer of my desk, I'd been able to connect the number Marsha Tederow had given M. J. McLeod to a house in the beach town of San Amaro. That was a few miles north of Malibu.

A sizable congregation of seagulls had gathered, huddling, out along the gray beach on my left and looking annoyed at the rain. Now and then a couple of them would rise up a few feet, wings flapping angrily, and start pecking at each other. From up ahead a flatbed truck full of freshly cut Christmas trees came roaring. Both the driver and his partner appeared to be wearing Santa hats.

"Hollywood," I muttered, "your magic spell is everywhere."

The drizzle segued into rain, the gray Pacific grew choppier.

My dashboard clock told me it was ten minutes after two, my wristwatch maintained it was only five minutes past, when I located Paloma Lane in San Amaro. It was a well-kept little street that held only six scattered houses on its three blocks. Number 232 had a high redwood fence around its half acre of land.

A high fence would come in handy if I had to break into Felix Denker's love nest.

Parking a half block from my target, I sat there for a few minutes. There didn't seem to be any outdoor activity in the vicinity and none of the houses was lit. I watched the ocean for a while, thinking about Jane and hoping that we'd both live to be extremely long in years and that I'd succeed in selling a movie script before our youngest child went off to college.

Then I eased free of the Ford and walked, very casually, up to the redwood fence. The narrow gate wasn't locked. Assuming an expression that indicated I had several—at least—perfectly legitimate reasons for prowling around here, I pushed it open to enter the yard.

There was a stretch of dry yellow lawn with a stone bench midway down on each side of the red flagstone path. The house looked to be about six or seven rooms, one story, and of the peach-colored stucco and red tile roof school of architecture. Chained to a rung of the ornamental iron porch rail was a bicycle, an expensive European woman's model.

The front door was locked. So was the back door.

I fished out the lock-pick kit that was a souvenir of my newspaper days and started fooling with the back door lock.

I got it unlocked. It led into the kitchen.

Something greenish brown in a casserole dish had spoiled in the icebox, which had used up its supply of ice several days earlier, I estimated.

A smell of strong tobacco lingered in the hall and all the other rooms of the hideaway. On the mantel of the small stone fireplace in the living room sat two framed photographs and a small snowing globe that held a portion of old Vienna within. The venetian blinds were closed tight and the flowered drapes drawn nearly shut.

I carried both pictures over to the floor lamp and clicked it on. One of the small photos showed the late Felix Denker, wearing his monocle, with his arm around a very pretty dark-haired girl in her middle twenties. One of the photos had been shot in the backyard and the other on a stretch of sunny after-noon beach. I couldn't tell whether someone else had taken them or if Denker had rigged a timing mechanism.

Assuming the young woman was Marsha Tederow, I slid the backyard photo out of its frame and dropped it into my breast pocket. The frames I returned to their original place over the fireplace.

The rain slapped hard against the windows while I poked

around the living room. There was a box of special-made cigarettes from "Van Gelder, Tobacconist" sitting on the glass-top coffee table next to a scatter of trade papers from a week or more earlier. Nothing in the fireplace, no scraps of paper or crumpled notes in the black wastebasket.

In the bedroom I found five dresses, three sweaters, and two pairs of slacks hanging in one of the closets. Marsha Tederow had also kept a small supply of lingerie, mostly white and frilly, in the middle drawer of the carved oaken bureau. Denker's drawer held a smattering of underwear, an ascot, and a carton of contraceptives. The only clothes of his in the closet were a crimson-and-gold silk dressing gown and what I took to be an old-fashioned striped nightgown.

On the nightstand on the side of the bed I figured had been the dead director's rested an empty coffee mug, a copy of a movie script for something titled *Death on a Dark Street*, and a monocle with a leather string attached.

In another closet was a blank stretched canvas, a pinewood box that held a barely touched set of expensive watercolors. Since Marsha Tederow had been an art director at Mammoth, I concluded she was the one who painted.

Leaning against the shadowy wall of the closet was a black leather portfolio of about the same dimensions as a page of the *L.A. Times*. Coaxing it out into the bedroom, I slapped the portfolio onto the unmade bed and unzipped it.

There were three rough charcoal sketches of Denker in thoughtful poses. Each had been signed "MT."

In a sleeve of the portfolio I discovered three books. One was a hardcover, the other two very thin paperbacks. I extracted them and carried them over to the dressing table, sat down, and clicked on the lamp.

They were in German. I studied Spanish in high school, French in college. Thing was, you didn't have to be a linguist to translate the titles or comprehend what they were about.

The hardcover was called something like *The Superiority of the Aryan Race*. The paperbacks were, approximately, *Why the Jew Is Inferior* and *How to Rid the Fatherland of the Curse of the Jews*. All three were the work of a Dr. Helga Krieger. In the front of the hardcover was a photo portrait of the author. Dr. Krieger, who was affiliated with a university in Munich in 1930 when all three of these works were published, was a fat, dark-haired woman in her late thirties. She wore a pince-nez and a self-satisfied expression.

I started to ask myself, "Why in the hell would Marsha Tederow save abysmal crap like this?"

I got as far as *abysmal*, when something took me by surprise.

What it was was a sudden sharp blow to the base of the skull.

I lost contact with everything at that point.

Twelve

● ● ● **r**eal horns of a dilemma, although, actually, now that I think about it, I'm not awfully certain why a dilemma should have horns in the first place, though that's probably beside the point in this instance and, certainly, I have to admit, that I haven't cured myself of the habit of straying, or at the very least wandering somewhat, from the point, and here's Frank Denby sprawled on the floor and I really would feel bad, no matter how much looking on the bright side I applied after the fact, if he came to grief because I neglected to take the appropriate action," someone was saying quite close to my head.

Speaking of my head, I was beginning to notice that it ached to a considerable degree.

I was sensing as well that whoever it was who was kneeling in my vicinity and delivering some sort of valedictory speech was someone I knew. A young woman I knew.

". . . calling the police, obviously, would be an absolutely fine thing to do, except that I really don't belong here at all and so they might get entirely too preoccupied with my trespassing, ignoring the fact, which isn't, I have to admit, a very valid legal premise, that since I was Marsha's roommate for nearly three months up in Beverly Glen, that I'm entitled to housebreak down here in San Amaro simply because she sometimes lived here with that odious man with the monocle and the slick hair, and, on top of that, Frank may be housebreaking, too, although now that he and Groucho are detecting once again, he may have a certain leeway when it comes to—"

"Victoria," I managed to cry out in a low, blurry voice.

I managed to persuade my left eye to open some.

Yellow lamplight came knifing in. I winced, groaned, and shut my eye.

"Are you conscious, Frank?" asked Victoria St. John, lips close to my ear. "Well, come to think of it, that's a pretty dippy question, because, obviously, if you were unconscious, this would be only a rhetorical question and—"

"Could you . . ." I took a slow breath in and out, then a slower one. "Could you maintain . . . perhaps . . . a moment of silence?"

"Well, certainly, it's not like I'm some chatterbox who just goes on ranting and raving for hours on end, especially when I've had a specific request to button my lip."

"Splendid," I muttered.

"I learned how to nurse injured people in relative silence and calm when I did volunteer work at the West Hollywood Clinic two years ago, although they finally asked me to do my volunteer work elsewhere because I was too distracting to some of the less stable patients, but that wasn't because of my admittedly sometimes excessive volubility. It was because the whole of Southern California seems to get inordinately overactive in the presence of a pretty blonde. But I'm probably talking too much again and, if there's one thing I learned at the clinic, it's to shut your yap around head wound victims.

Not that we had a great many people with head wounds wandering into the clinic, because, after all, it was West Hollywood and what you got more of was pokes in the snoot and . . . Well, you understand." She fell silent.

Either she fell silent or I passed out again. "Why are you here?" I was able to ask her after what might have been two or three minutes.

"It's going to seem like an enormous coincidence, but, to my way of thinking, there aren't really any coincidences but only odd juxtapositions of events and—"

"Victoria, I assume you aren't the one who bopped me on the coco," I cut in in a very creaky voice.

"Certainly not, Frank," she assured me, patting me, gingerly, between the shoulder blades. "I came here to snoop around and there you were, sprawled on the bedroom floor."

"You didn't see anybody?"

"Nary a soul," she answered. "Are you seriously injured, do you think? The bump on the back of your head didn't appear too awful, but then, unless I turned you over, there was no way I could tell if you didn't have more serious injuries."

With her help, I managed to sit up on the floor of the bedroom. When I stopped feeling dizzy, I asked her, "You were Marsha Tederow's roommate?"

Victoria nodded. "For nearly three months," she answered, tucking her legs under her and sitting close beside me. "Right after *Groucho Marx, Private Eye* left the air and, I'm sure I expressed this at the time last spring, but your discovering me right out of the blue working in that demeaning job as a Mullens Maiden and handing out samples of Mullens pudding, all five flavorful flavors, at grocery market openings and county fairs and even a Boy Scout jamboree, where I learned, by the way, that some of those scouts are very mature for their years, and giving me the chance to play Groucho's secretary on the Mullens pudding show was absolutely a wonderful gesture, and even though the show flopped the ninth week I was on it, it boosted my career immeasurably and I was able to get an agent, although Sid Gruber is not exactly the pinnacle of Hollywood agents, he did get me a nice regular part on *The Den of the Old Witch*, where I get to scream my heart out almost every week, and, what's more important to answering your question, I'm earning enough money to afford a nice place in Beverly Glen without having to wear a little short skirt and my front slit down to here."

"Am I correct in assuming that in that Icelandic epic you just recited, you didn't get around to explaining how you came to move in with Marsha Tederow?"

"I answered an ad in the *Hollywood Reporter.*"

When I nodded, to indicate that I understood, several new varieties of sharp pain went zigzagging through my skull. "And what brought you here to Denker's love nest?"

Victoria, who was wearing slacks and a sea-green pullover paused to collect her thoughts. "I've been making a very serious effort, Frank, to express myself concisely and I even attended a night school course in Westwood, except I found the instructor an awful windbag, which was odd in a way, since he claimed to have been an actor in silent movies, where, you'd have thought, he would've learned the value of . . . But, darn, I seem to be straying again," she realized. "Okay, here goes. When Marsha was killed in that terrible car accident, I assumed it was nothing more than an accident. But when Felix Denker got himself shot, that seemed to be stretching probability too far. There had to be some sort of connection, don't you think?

What I mean is, maybe Marsha was murdered, too, and they just made it look like an accident."

"I've been following up on a similar notion," I told her. "Any idea who might've wanted to kill her?"

Victoria said, "I got the impression over the last few weeks that Marsha was possibly involved in something shady."

"Shady how?"

"Well, one night when she'd had a couple of glasses of wine with dinner, she bragged to me that she was going to have a lot of money very soon."

"How was that going to happen?"

"She didn't provide any specific details, Frank. I suspect, though I hate to say this about anyone who was sort of a friend of mine, that Marsha was blackmailing somebody."

"You don't know who?"

Shaking her head, Victoria replied, "She never confided anything in me about it. My suspicion grew out of stuff I over-heard, just fragments of a couple of telephone conversations, and things I inferred."

"You expected to find something here?"

"I thought that if I could find anything pointing to whoever Marsha was trying to blackmail, that would give a pretty good idea of who killed her. That is, if she was murdered and they made it seem like an accident," Victoria said. "If I did come up with a substantial clue, I was planning to turn it over to you and Groucho to investigate, or, in a pinch, to the police."

I pressed the palm of my right hand to the floor, announc-ing, "I'm going to try to stand up."

The blonde got swiftly to her feet, took hold of my hand as I tottered upward. "If you feel woozy, holler."

"And then what?"

"Well, at least I'll know you're woozy."

I was able, with Victoria's help, to get myself seated on the bed. "Thanks," I said, and then noticed the portfolio. "The books. Look over on the dressing table—any books there?"

She crossed over, then shook her head and knelt. "Nothing on top and . . . nope, nothing on the floor either. What sort of books?"

"Hate literature is what I guess you'd have to call it. Three works by Dr. Helga Krieger—in German."

Victoria frowned, running her tongue over her upper lip. "I think I heard that name someplace."

"From your roommate?"

"Marsha didn't mention it to me directly, no, but I seem to recall hearing her say it once while she was on the telephone in the kitchen." She, slowly, shook her head. "Darn, I'm simply not sure, Frank. Is Dr. Helga Krieger a Nazi or something like that?"

"All I know so far is that she was living in Munich in 1930 and wrote some lousy books."

"The person who bopped you obviously swiped the books."

"Apparently so, yeah."

"That means they must be important."

"That it does, but thus far I haven't any idea why."

A frown touched her forehead. "I wonder if that's what they were looking for at our place, if, indeed, as I sort of suspected at the time, it was searched."

"Somebody searched your house?"

"I'm fairly certain, yes," she answered. "See, Frank, I came home from the radio studio the night after Marsha was killed, and, you know, I felt bad about performing so soon after her death but, show business being what it is, you have to go on

104

no matter what, especially with radio because you can't simply have dead air, although I suppose they could have rounded up somebody to fill in for me, and I got the distinct impression that somebody had been in the place. It was subtle, the furniture hadn't been tossed around or pictures taken off the wall, but things just didn't seem like they were exactly where they had been."

"You report it to the police?"

She shook her head. "Lots of people, especially of the official sort, tend to write me off as a scatterbrain," she answered. "So I didn't say anything to anybody, until now. But it's possible they were hunting for those same books."

"But you never saw anything like that around the house? Or anything else Marsha might've been hiding?"

"Not a thing, no, Frank, although, obviously, I had no reason to think the poor kid was hiding important books or documents, you know. It was only after Denker's murder that I really decided to do some snooping around. I didn't find anything at home, so I decided to come here."

I felt in the coat pocket where I'd earlier stowed the borrowed picture of Denker and the girl who was probably Marsha Tederow. Finding that the photo was still there, I took it out. "Would this be—"

"Look, here's your wallet." She reached over next to a leg of the dressing table and retrieved it.

I hadn't realized it had been removed. After she returned it to me, I checked the contents. I still had my thirty-seven dollars in cash and all my identification and the strip of photos of Jane and me we'd taken at a penny arcade last summer. "Well, now the Phantom knows who I am, even including how much I weigh and what my Social Security number is," I reflected, sticking the wallet back in my hip pocket. "He may, of course, have known that already."

"Where'd you get that picture of Marsha and the weasel?"

"Mantel up in the living room. It is her?"

Victoria had picked up the photo I'd dropped to the bedspread when she handed me my wallet. "Yes, that's Marsha with Denker," she answered quietly. "I know you're supposed to speak well of the dead, but I believe that everything bad that happened to her was his fault."

I took the picture back, asking, "Can you do me a favor?"

"Hush up, you mean?"

"No, it's that I'd like to try to drive home to our place in Bayside. You got here in a car?"

"Yes, and I can give you a lift home. That'd be much safer than my trailing you all the way to Bayside to make sure—"

"I'm reluctant to leave my Ford sitting here until I can arrange to come back for it."

"Okay," she said, holding out her hand again. "I'll get you tucked into your car and then tag along behind you."

"That's swell, Victoria."

"If you feel at all woozy or dizzy or poorly in any way while you're driving, simply stick your hand out the window and wave, or if you're too weak to do that, toot your horn. If you're not up even to that, I'll just have to wait until you careen off the road and hope for the best and that I can get there before you do serious harm to yourself."

"That's very thoughtful."

Our caravan made it home without my careening off the road once.

Thirteen

This is quite a treat," Groucho told the hovering British actor, "getting to meet the Giant Rat of Sumatra in person like this. Any red-blooded Conan Doyle fan would envy me."

"If only your own obvious appreciation of your inane remarks were shared by the world, my dear Groucho, you'd be a clever man indeed." Uninvited, the slender, vaguely handsome Miles Ravenshaw seated himself opposite Groucho and took a puff of his meerschaum pipe.

"Do they know at Mammoth that you're bringing your Sherlock Holmes props home from work, Ravenshaw?"

Before the actor could respond, a waiter had trotted over to ask, "Will the gentleman be joining you, Mr. Marx?"

"No, and neither will Mr. Ravenshaw." Groucho tapped the menu. "My appetite, alas, has seriously faded. I do believe I'll simply have a bowl of soup."

"We have beef barley and chicken noodle."

"I'll try the chicken noodle."

"Very good, sir." The long, thin waiter jotted down the order, bowed, and started walking away.

Groucho called after him, "Quick, Watson, the noodle."

Ravenshaw exhaled smoke. "I hope you understand, my dear fellow, that such crude—"

"Does your valet have to iron your profile every morning to get it to look like that?"

"When I noticed you sitting here, I stepped over to pass along some advice."

Holding up his right hand in a stop-right-there gesture, Groucho suggested, "What say we have a man-to-man discussion? And, yes, I'll wait until you go out and get a man to represent you."

"Frankly, Groucho, your—"

"Here's the sum total of what I have to say to you at this time." Groucho rested both elbows on the tabletop. "I don't believe you give a damn about who killed Felix Denker or about seeing justice done. You're in this solely to promote *The Valley of Fear.*"

"Ah, yes, and I suppose your motives are noble and completely unselfish."

"They are indeed, Shylock. I'm interested in furthering the cause of a deserving group of unemployed vaudevillians."

"You're dead wrong about me, Groucho," the actor assured him. "As a former Scotland Yard inspector, with considerable experience in murder investigations, I know I can solve the murder of Felix Denker. And, frankly, I shall accomplish that before the police do." He leaned forward, holding his thumb and forefinger about an inch apart. "I can safely state, my dear fellow, that I am this far from a solution."

"Congratulations, it isn't every man who's as close as his own putz length to solving a murder case."

Bestowing a disdainful expression on Groucho, the actor said, "Your so-called droll remarks are growing exceedingly—"

"How about a picture, fellows?" A pudgy young man with a camera had stopped beside the booth. "I'm with the Associated Press and a photo of you two friendly rivals having a powwow will—"

"Oh, dear, I fear not," said Groucho demurely. "As a dedicated disciple of both Mahatma Gandhi and Greta Garbo, I shun the limelight and passively avoid all forms of vulgar publicity."

"C'mon, Groucho, you know damned well that—"

"Well, perhaps merely one fleeting shot, young man," he conceded. "But, mind you now, see to it that it's not too flattering and do try to arrange things so that I don't come out looking too much more dazzlingly cute than Mr. Ravenshaw. You might also want to make certain that Mr. Ravenshaw doesn't look too much like John Barrymore again, because that's simply going to lead to another of those annoying plagiarism suits. For myself—"

"My dear Groucho, do allow this long-suffering young chap to take our photograph, won't you, please? After that, I can, having done my best to dissuade you from your path of folly, take my leave and—"

"Of course, yes, forgive my schoolgirl prattle." Groucho smoothed out the front of his jacket. "Be sure you bring out the sparkle in my eyes."

Grinning, the photographer backed a few feet and readied his camera.

A few seconds before he was about to shoot, the waiter returned with Groucho's bowl of chicken noodle soup.

At that same instant, Groucho decided to hop up and seat himself on the edge of the table with both hands locked under his chin in a cherubic pose. Somehow his elbow managed to whap the soup bowl and send its steaming contents splashing down into Ravenshaw's lap.

Looking both stunned and uncomfortable, the Holmes impersonator started to leap up off his seat.

That scene was the one that went out on the AP wire across the country that afternoon.

Before returning to his Cadillac, Groucho decided to stop at a small cigar store to use the telephone.

He was about ten feet from the narrow doorway when a plump middle-aged woman stepped into his path. Lurking to her rear, clutching a box camera, was a plump middle-aged man.

"Mr. Marx, would you pose with me?" she requested

He halted and stroked his chin thoughtfully. "By jingo, that's a top-notch suggestion," he said, starting to undo his necktie. "There's nothing I enjoy better than posing in the nude."

Holding up both hands in front of her, she took a step back. "No, no, I meant just pose for a snapshot."

"It doesn't have to be an oil painting, dear lady," he assured her. "I'm equally happy to pose for a nude snapshot. Come along now, start shedding those garments."

"I'm afraid I got off on the wrong foot," she said, glancing over toward her husband. "All I want is a simple snapshot of you and me standing side by side. Fully clothed."

Looking disappointed, Groucho said, "Well, okay, if you've gotten cold feet. And, from what you've just told me, they're the wrong cold feet at that."

Cautiously, she moved near to him again. "I truly appreciate this, Mr. Marx," she said. "I'm a real admirer of the Marx Brothers."

"Could I interest you in some nude photos of the whole set of them?"

Inside the cigar store, Groucho stepped up to the counter. "Give me a couple of Don José cigars," he told the small, pale proprietor.

"Those are expensive. Cost you four bits each."

"I can afford it. I just won the Yiddish Sweepstakes."

The man handed him an open box of cigars. "Don't I know you?"

"Quite probably. I'm the Lost Dauphin of France."

"No, you're Groucho Marx."

"You think so? Darn, that means I've been wearing this uncomfortable iron mask for naught all these years." He selected two cigars, placed a dollar bill on the glass countertop. "And you should see what naught's been wearing for me."

"Can I ask you something, Groucho?"

"As long as it doesn't involve my steamy sex life or the capitals of the states."

"How come you guys made a clunker like *Room Service*?"

"It's part of a religious rite known as penance," explained Groucho as he tucked the cigars away in the breast pocket of his jacket. "They promised us that if we made that movie, why, ten thousand suffering souls would be released from purgatory." He consulted his wristwatch. "And, now, with considerable reluctance, I'm going to bid you fond farewell and journey over to that phone booth yonder."

"Be my guest, Groucho."

Inside the booth, he first called the office of his brother Zeppo.

"Good afternoon, brother mine, this is your favorite sibling and . . . What do you mean, it doesn't sound like Chico? It is I, the incomparable Julius, who . . . No, I'm definitely not comparable. Now then, Zep, to business and . . . Of course, I have time for purely sociable conversation. How are you? Good, now then . . . I didn't know you had a sore throat, or I would've inquired about it. I was saying just the other evening to Louella Parsons, while she was modeling some of her latest winter underwear for me and Willie Hearst, that if there was one thing in this cockeyed world I was truly interested in, it was my youngest brother's throat. So how's your throat already? . . . No, I'm sincerely interested. Better, huh? Well sir, there's the sort of news that'll cheer the boys at the front and, I'll wager, make Kaiser Bill think twice about . . . Straying from the point? I've had the point clearly in mind ever since I wandered into this phone kiosk several hours ago and . . . Well, actually, Zeppo, I'd like you to do me a small favor. What I . . . No, that's certainly not true. I don't just telephone you when I want a favor. If you'll think back to the year 1911, you'll recall that I telephoned you to say nothing more than that I had spilled soup on that vest of yours I'd borrowed to wear to the Harvest Moon Ball. I distinctly . . . the favor? You have, because of your activities as an internationally successful talent agent, contacts in London. I'd appreciate it if you would contact a reliable source over there and see what you can come up with on Miles Ravenshaw. He claims to . . . You do? Well, thank you. Yes, it should provide some nice publicity for me and Frank and our proposed screwball comedy. But I really do want to solve this damn case. Anything you can dig up about Ravenshaw's association with Scotland Yard, scandals, feuds, possible prior connections with Felix Denker or Erika Klein, will be greatly appreciated and . . . I know it's expensive to phone or cable London. That's exactly why I'm turning to my most solvent sibling. I'll let you get going on the project, Zeppo."

Dropping in another nickel, he dialed his office.

"Groucho Marx Enterprises," answered Nan.

"This is Julius the Magnificent. I seem to be suffering from partial amnesia and can't remember what comes after *hocus.* Can you suggest—"

"Quit clowning. Frank's been hurt."

"How seriously?"

"He'll be okay. Poor guy got slugged by somebody with a blackjack."

"Where is he?"

"Home, with Jane taking care of him," she answered. "She just had a doctor in looking him over and he's going to be okay. But he has to rest up for a day or so."

"I called to tell you I was planning to head out to Altadena Community College next," Groucho said to his secretary. "But this alters things. I'll scoot over to Frank's."

"That would be the thoughtful thing to do."

"Okay, but don't go blabbing to anybody that I actually did something thoughtful." He hung up.

Fourteen

When Jane opened our front door, a large floral horseshoe came walking in out of the waning afternoon. The banner across its front proclaimed *Lots of Luck with Your Kosher Butcher Shop!*

Carrying the flower piece across the living room and draping it on an arm of the sofa I was reclining on, Groucho explained, "This was the closest thing I could find to 'Sorry you got conked on the noggin in the line of duty' at the day-old florist shop. There was an awfully nice wreath of yellow roses, but it read 'Rest in Peace, Aunt Edith, from the Amalgamated Tool and Die Craftsmen.' That struck me as a trifle morbid."

"It's the thought that counts," I assured him, sitting up.

He leaned close, stretching in an attempt to get a look at the back of my head. "Nan informs me you're not seriously incapacitated."

"A minor concussion," I said. "The blow was sufficient to knock me cold, but it didn't do any major damage."

"It could've, though," said Jane, gathering up the flower piece and carrying it over to lean against the wall. "You fellows have barely started investigating this business and already Frank's getting bopped on the head."

I said, "It's okay, Jane, you and I have already talked about this and—"

"I'm not nagging," she said. "What I'm doing is reminding you two Junior G-Men that you're messing around with something serious."

"You're absolutely right, Jane." Groucho settled into an armchair. "And I have to admit that I wasn't expecting your hubby to be attacked so early in the game. Usually he doesn't get coldcocked until the third or fourth day of the—"

"What say," I suggested, "we quit chatting about my stupidity and compare notes on—"

"You weren't stupid because somebody snuck up on you." Jane joined me on the sofa.

"Careless, then," I said.

Groucho asked, "Any idea who it was that did the deed?"

When I gave a negative shake of my head, some flashes of sharp pain struck at the back of my neck. "Nope, Groucho."

"Even more to the point, where were you exactly when the attack took place?"

I told him about the love nest in San Amaro and about finding the anti-Semitic books that Marsha Tederow had apparently hidden away there.

"Dr. Helga Krieger," he said slowly when I finished. "Never heard of the dear lady, I'll be sure to inquire after her when I call on Professor Hoffman tomorrow."

"It could be the books had some connection with a blackmail scheme Marsha was trying to work," I suggested.

Cupping his hand to his ear, Groucho said, "Eh, how's that? Did I fail to hear the juicy details about a blackmail plot?"

116

"Hadn't gotten to that yet." I proceeded to fill him in on what I'd learned from my encounter with Victoria St. John. "So if Marsha was blackmailing somebody, then her death probably wasn't accidental."

"Victoria St. John." Groucho rolled his eyes. "I don't suppose she was still wearing her skimpy Mullens Maiden uniform?"

"Nope."

"A pity." Groucho stretched up out of the chair, scratched at his ribs, and commenced pacing in his bent-knee way. "You're certain it wasn't the fair Vicky who crept up and slugged you, Rollo?"

"She's incapable of sneaking up on anybody, and besides I trust her."

Jane sighed, saying nothing.

"That would seem to indicate that three different people descended on that little hideaway at about the same time," Groucho pointed out. "Why?"

"In my case, it was because I only just found out about it."

Jane said, "Somebody may've followed Frank. Picked him up after he met with his old girlfriend, Mary Jane."

"Possibly," agreed Groucho, unwrapping a Don José cigar as he paced. "Or, like Frank, they just today found out about the joint and rushed there to snoop around."

"Far as I can tell, they only swiped those Nazi books," I said. "Meaning that stuff has to tie in somehow."

"There are a couple of possibilities." He put the cigar in his mouth but didn't bother to light it. "Those specific copies may be of value to somebody—contain hidden messages in code or incriminating marginal notes. Or Dr. Helga herself is connected with the murders in some way."

"Murders plural?" asked Jane. "You agree that Marsha Tederow was murdered?"

He nodded. "For the moment, yes indeedy," he answered. "Let's say she was blackmailing someone linked with the Dr. Helga tomes. They decide to fake her murder to seem an accident and eliminate that threat. They kill her, search her home, and find nothing. Later, upon learning that she also had spent some time in San Amaro, they arrive at that cozy locale just in time to render the intrepid Franklin unconscious and grab the stuff."

"You got a brief look at a picture of Dr. Krieger," Jane reminded me. "What'd she look like?"

I thought about that. "Well, not like anybody we've run into on this case thus far," I answered finally. "Pudgy lady, probably weighs about two hundred pounds, plain-looking. Dark hair, pulled back in a bun. Spectacles on her nose, nose wide and flat. She'd be in her middle forties or thereabouts now."

Groucho sat down again. "Now then, what did you learn out at Mammoth this morning?"

"Mainly, sir, that we're personas non grata," I informed him. "We're not to be allowed on the studio premises until after Ravenshaw solves the case."

"I always get *personas non grata* mixed up with *potatoes au gratin*," admitted Groucho. "Which makes for some unusual moments when it comes time to order my meals. Who barred us from the lot, Lew Number One himself?"

"Yeah, but Randy Grothkopf in Publicity put him up to it."

"One more reason to beat all these other schlemiels to the punch and catch the killer," he pointed out. "Otherwise we can't get back inside the lot to sell *Cinderella on Wheels* to Lew Number Two."

Jane looked from Groucho to me. "Okay, any idea so far who did kill Denker or the Tederow girl?"

Groucho replied, "Well, it wasn't Franz Henkel, the Nazi stagehand."

"The police seem to think it was Henkel," I put in.

"So does the tear-soaked widow," Groucho said, and went on to give us an account of what had taken place during his visit with Erika Klein at Merlinwood.

"Threatening letters can be very convincing evidence," observed Jane when he'd concluded.

"Okay, Franz Henkel might be somebody's stooge," he conceded, "but he doesn't sound like the sort of lad who'd be getting himself blackmailed because of a supposed connection with Dr. Helga Krieger. And, B movies to the contrary, really first-rate villains don't often send threatening letters to people they intend to bump off."

"Sergeant Norment doesn't seem to agree," my wife said.

"We don't really know what the sarge thinks about anything," said Groucho. "He's not sharing much with the newspapers and even less with us. For example, I've heard nary a word about that sleeping authoress we encountered in that quaint little British pub yesterday."

"I found out something about Clair Rickson, although I'm not sure I believe some of it," I said, and filled him in on what I'd pried out of Mary Jane. "I should be able to find out which sanitarium she's stowed in and sneak in for a chat."

"Yes, jot that on your list of good deeds to do, Rollo."

"Also be interesting to know what our local Sherlock Holmes is up to," I said.

Groucho sat up, smiling. "There I can help out, my dears," he said, and recounted his adventures at Musso and Frank's.

"Remind me to clip out a copy of that picture for my memory book, when and if it appears."

Jane put her hand on my shoulder. "You're starting to look a little tired, Frank."

"I'm okay," I lied. Actually I was beginning to feel somewhat weary.

To Groucho she said, "Sounds to me like Ravenshaw isn't really putting much of an effort into this. It's probably all bluff and public relations crap."

"I've always thought the man was a halfwit, but I don't want to screw up things by underestimating him," Groucho answered. "Maybe he is only an inch away from the answer." He shrugged. "I doubt it, however." He left his chair again. "Tomorrow I'll call on Professor Hoffman out at Altadena Community College and see where that leads me."

"I'll try to get a copy of the accident report on Marsha Tederow in the morning," I said. "And I can check with a couple of informants for news of where Franz Henkel may be holed up."

"In the afternoon maybe you'll do that," corrected Jane. "In the morning you are going to rest."

"In the afternoon I'll do that, Groucho."

He wandered in the direction of the door. "I must tear myself away from all this domestic bliss," he said. "When you're through with the flowers, Frank, let me know. There's a kosher meat market I think I can unload them on."

Fifteen

Groucho made rather slow progress across the campus of Altadena Community College the next morning.

Altadena is a town that lies just above Pasadena and he arrived at the visitors' parking lot at about ten minutes shy of ten, parked his Cadillac, and started hiking toward the building that housed the German lit department. The college covered roughly fifteen acres and was in the traditional red brick and abundant ivy mold, with winding paths, rolling lawns, and an occasional tree-filled glade.

Just inside the arched wrought-iron entry gates several card tables had been set up, manned by students representing such organizations as the Young People's Socialist League, the Cinema Club, the China Relief Fund, and the World Federalists.

Groucho stopped for a moment at the WF table to pick up a pamphlet.

As he was moving away, a young man in sweater and slacks noticed him and exclaimed, "Groucho Marx! What are you doing here?"

Resting one foot on a pathside bench, Groucho answered, "That's a most interesting story, young feller. It all began when my mother entrusted me with the selling of the family cow. Well sir, I'd been intending to schlep old Bossy over to a used cow lot in Burbank, but then I ran into a man with a hand full of beans. Yes, I know, that sounds messy, but he—"

"It's Groucho!" cried a blond coed in a checkered skirt, cashmere sweater, and saddle shoes as she joined the growing group near the bench.

"What the heck are you doing at ACC?" asked a husky young man in a letter sweater.

"It all began," Groucho began again, "when we set sail from Dover in the year of our Lord—"

"Do you do your own singing in the movies or is it dubbed?" This from a plump redheaded girl who'd bumped the number of surrounding students up to roughly thirty.

"I do all my own singing, yes," answered Groucho. "My talking, however, is dubbed by Charles Boyer. Or, on days when he has to work late at the fish market, by Bobby Breen."

"I read somewhere," said a freshly arrived coed, "that you used to be a tenor in vaudeville."

"No, my child, I was a tenor with the Metropolitan Opera," corrected Groucho. "I was, in fact, the first tenor to sing the part of Kate Smith in *I Have Madame Butterflies in My Stomach*."

"What's Clark Gable really like?"

"Very much like me. Except his ears are smaller."

"Did you ever date Norma Shearer?"

"No."

"What famous actresses have you gone out with?"

"I once had an interesting encounter with Joan Crawford in a telephone booth in Tijuana," Groucho answered. "I cannot, alas, share the story with you because I sold the exclusive rights to the *Wrestling News* just yesterday."

"Why doesn't Harpo talk in your movies?"

"Harpo does talk, but at a pitch that only dogs can hear. Ask your Saint Bernard friends and see if I'm not absolutely right."

"What's your favorite role?"

"Now, there, young lady, is a question I can really sink my teeth into. I—"

"Please, you're not going to answer, 'A poppy-seed roll,' or something dumb like that?"

Groucho took on a sheepish expression, digging the toe of his right shoe into the sward. "Gosh, I plumb forgot I was trapped in the midst of an intellectual crowd and that my low-brow japes wouldn't cut the mustard here," he admitted rue-fully. "I was intending to reply either with 'a kaiser roll' or, at the risk of bringing down the wrath of the Watch and Ward Society, 'a roll in the hay.' "

The small dark coed asked, "You are capable of giving a serious answer, aren't you?"

Poking his tongue into his cheek, Groucho gazed upward into the clear blue morning sky. "Okay, kiddo, here's a completely straight answer," he said. "I really get a kick out of pretending to be Groucho Marx."

The campus bell tower sounded the hour of ten. By that time there were more than a hundred students surrounding Groucho.

"I must be going," he announced, starting to work his way clear of the bench.

"Are you smarter than Sherlock Holmes?" someone called after him as he headed uphill.

"That," he responded, "remains to be seen."

While Groucho was delivering his sermon to the multitudes, I was taking a solitary walk along the morning Pacific.

I'd been able to sneak a few telephone calls, but then Jane had emerged from her studio and caught me in the act of persuading a former *L.A. Times* colleague to rustle me up a copy of the official report on Marsha Tederow's automobile accident.

As soon as I cradled the receiver she said, "You've still got several more hours of recuperating to do, remember?"

"Nope, apparently memory lapses are one of my symptoms."

Making an impatient noise, she pointed at the living room door. "Go out and stroll along the beach," she advised. "It's rumored to be beneficial."

"Sitting on my backside using a telephone isn't that strenuous or—"

"Soon as high noon rolls around, you can get back into your gumshoes."

"You have a spot of ink on the tip of your nose."

"Undoubtedly. Go take a hike."

"Mutter, mutter," I said, rising from the sofa.

"So you've located a copy of that accident report?" she asked as I reached for the doorknob.

"Should have one by late this afternoon, yeah."

"And the whereabouts of Franz Henkel?"

"Got an appointment to talk to an old informant of mine at three down in L.A." I stepped out into the bright, warm December morning.

Our present house was less than five minutes uphill from the ocean.

Someone had built a pretty impressive sand castle just beyond the furthest reach of the surf. There were six turrets and a drawbridge. Standing alone in the courtyard was a solitary lead soldier in the uniform of the Chinese army.

Squatting momentarily, I scooped him up and dropped him into my trouser pocket.

Far ahead of me on the beach a heavyset woman in a long yellow terry cloth robe was standing wide-legged, hands on hips, calling something that sounded like, "Rasputin! Rasputin!"

Long before I reached her vicinity, I found a large twist of driftwood that looked suitable for sitting. I seated myself, staring out to sea.

I was still there fifteen minutes later when Jane tracked me down.

"I figure that if we sail in that direction," I told her, pointing toward the hazy horizon, "we should be able to establish a new trade route to the Orient."

"That's the same darn thing Marco Polo told me the last time we had dinner."

"I don't like dining with that bozo anymore. He only wants to go to chop suey joints."

"You just got a phone call from Victoria St. John." Bending slightly, she held out her hand to me.

I caught hold and pulled myself upright. "Something important?"

"Sounded so to me, yes," she replied. "Victoria says that when she was cleaning house this morning, she came across a memo slip that had gotten lost under a throw rug. She's pretty certain it's the note Marsha made about where she was supposed to go the night she was killed."

125

"Great—who was she scheduled to meet?"

"According to your erstwhile Mullens Maiden, there's nobody's name listed," Jane explained. "And keep in mind that what I'm giving you is based on my having to winnow a substantial, circumlocutious conversation, replete with footnotes and asides, from Victoria. The gist is—Marsha was heading for a bar over in Sherman Oaks. Place is called the Cutting Room and she was to meet somebody there at ten P.M. that Thursday night."

"Never heard of the place."

"Neither had Victoria, but she looked it up in the telephone book and provided us with an address."

Nodding, I took hold of Jane's arm as we started uphill toward our beach house. "I'll drive over there this afternoon."

"I'd like to tag along, Frank."

"You caught up on your comic strip deadlines?"

"I am. Fact is, I'm even ahead on my Sunday page schedule."

I eyed her. "You simply want to help out on this—or is this a move to keep me from getting together with Victoria?"

"Both," she admitted.

Sixteen

Professor Ernst Hoffman was a small, neat man in his middle fifties. His office was small, neat, and devoid of clutter. Most of the books on the shelves that covered two of the walls were in German and a bust of Goethe sat atop the wooden filing cabinet.

As Groucho settled into a straight-back chair next to his rolltop desk, Hoffman leaned to plant a heavy cut-glass ashtray on his knee. "For your cigar, Julius."

"It's not lit, Ernie."

"Should you, my friend, decide to light it."

Removing the unlit cigar from between his teeth, Groucho dropped it into a side pocket of his sports coat. He returned the ashtray to the professor. "Now, what I'd—"

"That's not sanitary, stowing that cigar butt in there like that."

"It's okay, Professor. The pastrami sandwich is wrapped in wax paper, so the stogie won't contaminate it. Although, now that I think about it, the kosher dill may get a little fragrant."

Hoffman frowned for a few seconds. "Ah, I keep forgetting

that you're a comedian," he said, chuckling and placing the ashtray two inches to the left of his fountain pen.

"Millions of people had the same problem while witnessing *Room Service.*"

"I rarely go to the movies these days. In Berlin it was different and I found the films made by people like Fritz Lang and Felix Denker were—"

"When did you talk to Denker last?"

The professor straightened up. "You actually are investigating his death?"

Groucho nodded. "The police have indicated they think that a disgruntled stagehand named Franz Henkel may have killed Denker," he said. "Did Denker ever mention him to you?"

Pushing back from his desk, Hoffman crossed to the filing cabinet to tug out the middle door partway. "Henkel is active in the German American Bund, Julius, and he was a Nazi bully-boy in Munich until he came to America something like three years ago." Extracting a manila folder he handed it to Groucho. "I like to keep up with people like Henkel."

There was a small photograph of a thickset man, crew cut and wearing a tight-fitting black suit, clipped to the two pages of typed information about Franz Henkel. After skimming the material, Groucho closed the folder. "Henkel sounds like an errand boy to me," he said. "Not the sort of lad to plan and carry out an assassination."

"He might have beaten up Felix on a dark street someplace, but no, he hasn't the nerve or the brains for murder."

"Did Denker really have him fired from Mammoth?"

Professor Hoffman nodded. "Oh, yes," he answered. "But not, as has been hinted in the press, because of threats. Felix remembered Henkel from Germany and refused to have the man working on any film of his. He had enough influence at the studio to get the union to agree to removing him."

"The only address you have on the guy is the one the police let out," Groucho observed. "No idea where he's presently holed up?"

"I'm trying to find out, but as of today, no, Julius," said Hoffman, taking the folder back from him and setting it three inches to the left of the ashtray. "It's possible that Henkel does know something about who killed Felix."

"Okay, why do you think Denker was killed?"

The professor rubbed his hands together slowly. "Something was bothering him, but he didn't confide what," he said. "I saw him for dinner last week and it was evident he was worried about something."

"When?"

"It was Friday evening. We met at a Mexican restaurant down near the Union Station, on Figueroa Street."

"Did he talk about Marsha Tederow?"

The professor said, "You know about that affair?"

Groucho nodded. "He seems to have set up a little hideaway in the town of San Amaro where they could meet on the sly," he said.

"Felix was, quite obviously, very upset over her death," Hoffman said. "In fact, I believe he asked me to dinner because he had intended to talk about her, tell me something about her death." He shook his head. "Then he seemed to change his mind—implied he wasn't ready. He did say that he felt her death was, in some way, his responsibility."

"He didn't kill her, did he?"

"You suspect it wasn't an accident?"

"Seems unlikely that it could've been."

129

Professor Hoffman said, "No, his feelings of guilt about Marsha's death weren't because he'd actually killed her. He did, however, feel responsible."

"How?"

"That he decided not to talk about."

"You knew both Denker and Erika Klein in Germany," said Groucho. "Were they a devoted couple then or—"

"I only met Erika once or twice in Berlin," said Hoffman. "Felix married her only a few months before emigrating. I never felt they were especially close and really . . ." He made a dismissive gesture and stopped talking.

Groucho leaned forward. "What? I can use all the background stuff you've got, Ernie."

After rubbing his hands together again, the professor said, "Felix changed quite a bit after arriving in America. In Germany, for at least two years before he left, he was a very serious gambler. Dedicated to it the way only men who continually lose are."

"The guy was in hock?"

"Quite a bit, yes, Julius. But then, shortly before he married, he was able to settle all this gambling debts."

Groucho's left eyebrow climbed. "You think Erika's family came up with a dowry for Denker?"

"I never asked and I don't even know if her people were wealthy," he answered. "Yet it did strike me as an interesting coincidence, you know."

"Erika wasn't especially jealous of her husband, from what I've heard."

"Felix wasn't killed because he was unfaithful to his wife, no."

The phone on the professor's neat desktop rang. "Yes, Hoffman here." After listening for a moment, he smiled and handed the receiver to Groucho. "Your secretary, Julius."

"Hello, Nanook. Didn't I tell you never to telephone me when I'm at a bordello or a college?"

"You just got an interesting phone call."

"Really? And how did I react to that?"

"British actor named Randell McGowan is very eager to talk to you," explained Nan. "He says he'll be at the Britannia Club in Beverly Hills from three until five this afternoon. Know where that is?"

"Indeed I do. I've been turned away from their front doors on three separate occasions and twice from the tradesmen's entrance," he said, rubbing at his chin with his free hand. "McGowan, if memory serves, is the chap who's portraying Dr. Watson to Ravenshaw's Holmes, is he not?"

"That's the boy, yeah," answered his secretary. "Apparently he and Ravenshaw aren't exactly what you'd call bosom buddies. What he told me was that he just remembered something that has to do with the Denker murder and he'll be damned if he'll give it to that rotter Ravenshaw. And he's too much of a gentleman to deal directly with the police."

"Ah, so that leaves me, the lesser of two rotters."

"Can you meet him, Groucho? He sounded legit."

"Most British actors sound that way. I almost bought a secondhand car off Eric Blore once," Groucho said. "But, sure, I'll pop into the Britannia. Anything else new? Any orphans left on the doorstep?"

"None worth keeping. Bye."

"Excuse the interruption," said Groucho.

"So you're really in a competition with this Sherlock Holmes actor, are you?"

"I am, even though it adds a cheesy aspect to the case."

"It's all right, Julius, so long as you find out who killed Felix."

He asked the professor, "Did Denker ever mention a Dr. Helga Krieger to you, Ernie?"

"How'd you come to hear of her?"

Groucho explained about the books I'd momentarily found at the love nest. "Was she someone Denker and Erika knew over there?"

"I don't believe so, and Felix never alluded to her so far as I can recall," answered Hoffman. "But I heard quite a bit about her, while I was teaching in Munich."

"An anti-Semitic lady, as I understand it."

"Dr. Krieger was one of several Aryan scholars, someone who worked full-time to prove that Germans were superior to anyone else and, worse, that the stock had to be kept pure," he explained, picking up his pen and tapping angrily with it on the blotter as he spoke. "She also lectured at rallies and meetings of political clubs. A Nazi bitch through and through."

"What happened to her?"

"One hopes she's dead and rotting in a grave someplace in Germany," he said. "She dropped from sight in the early 1930s. New material from her ceased to appear in the Nazi press and the personal appearances simply ended."

"Could she be in America?"

Professor Hoffman studied the ceiling. "If she is, I've never heard a word about it," he said finally. "And, as you know, I keep up with things like that."

"So why would three books by her be so important?"

The professor gave a negative shake of his head. "I have no idea, my friend. It's possible they have some other value, something that has nothing to do directly with Dr. Krieger."

"That's occurred to me, too, but I have this hunch that Dr. Helga is more directly tied in with what's been going on."

"Hunches are fine in their place, but what you need to solve this mystery are facts, Julius."

Nodding, he stood up. "Thanks for reminding me, Ernie," he said, backing toward the door. "I'd better go round up some more."

Seventeen

Every surface of the Cutting Room that could be covered with knotty pine was. The small barroom sat on the edge of an unpaved parking lot and its blue-tinted side windows gave you a view of weedy fields and a patch of woodlands. Behind the narrow bar hung a large framed linen movie poster featuring Guy Pope in the part of Ivanhoe. The bartender, a thickset bearded man in a faded UCLA sweatshirt, was absently polishing glasses and watching a buzzing fly avoid getting caught on a dangling strip of flypaper.

Jane and I had barely crossed the threshold and the scents of stale beer and old cigarette smoke had just commenced engulfing us, when three midgets in dark business suits stood up at a table on our left and all waved.

The midget with the mustache called out, "Hiya, Janey, honey."

The midget wearing the horn-rimmed glasses inquired, "How's by you, toots?"

The third midget, who was about six inches shorter than his colleagues, was red-haired and freckled. He came hurrying over and held out his hand to me. "Put her there, pal," he invited. "You must be Janey's old man."

"It's the Spiegelman Brothers," she explained to me as she smiled at them with restrained enthusiasm.

"The Spiegelman Brothers?" I inquired while shaking hands.

"We're better known in the east," said the one I was shaking hands with. "I'm Leroy."

"They're not really brothers, except for show business purposes." Jane waved at the two who'd remained at the table with their drinks. "Hi, Edwin. Hi, Mort."

"So you guys are in show business, huh?" I said to Leroy.

"You thought maybe we were a trio of undersized insurance salesmen?"

"I met the Spiegelman Brothers about a year ago," explained Jane as we headed for the bar. "RKO was thinking about making some comedy shorts based on the *Hillbilly Willy* comic strip and the Spiegelman boys were going to play the Moonshine Triplets."

"Louella Parsons and Johnny Whistler never mentioned that, so I was unaware of—"

"You still out of work?" asked Leroy, who'd stuck with us.

"I'm between pictures."

"You have to have written a picture first, buster, before you can be between them."

"I'm between scripts, then."

"That radio show you did with Groucho wasn't too terrible," conceded Leroy.

Jane tapped him on the shoulder. "It's been nice running into you boys again, but right now—"

"You'd appreciate it if I did a scramola?"

"We're actually sort of here on business and—"

"No need to apologize, Janey." Reaching up, Leroy patted my wife on her left buttock and, smiling up at me, went trotting back to rejoin the other Spiegelman Brothers.

"They took a liking to me." Jane perched on a stool at the bar.

"Don't let those little peckerheads annoy you," advised the bearded bartender. "This is their favorite hangout at the moment. Soon as they get work again things'll get back to normal."

There were no other customers in the place.

"They think it's funny to order Napoléon brandy," he said. "What'll you folks have?"

I glanced at Jane, who shrugged one shoulder. "Couple of beers," I said.

"Care which kind?"

"Not especially."

"Myself, I'm partial to Rainier."

"That'll do, sure."

After he brought the bottles and glasses and I'd paid him, I fished out the copy of my expired *Los Angeles Times* press card that I still carried around with me. Then I took out the picture of Marsha Tederow and Felix Denker I'd borrowed at the love nest the day before.

After providing the bartender a very brief look at the defunct card, I placed the photo on the bar facing toward him. "Doing a follow-up story," I explained. "Ever see these people?"

He picked up the photograph, brought it up close to his face. "Sure, yeah."

"When were they in here last?"

He shook his shaggy head. "Far as I know they've never been in the Cutting Room."

"But you know them?"

"Not the dame, no. The guy, though, is Felix Denker, the director who got bumped off yesterday," he answered. "I had a bit part in his *Lynch Mob*. I was one of the rowdies carrying a coil of rope in the scenes where—"

"What about the girl?" asked Jane. "Sure she wasn't in here last week one night?"

He looked at her and not the photo. "You with the *Times*, too, sister?"

"Matter of fact, I am, yeah," she replied. "Right now I'm his girl Friday. So?"

"I only work weekend nights and I don't remember—"

"Who would've been on duty last Thursday?" I asked.

"That the dame got herself killed in that car wreck last week?" Leroy had come back over from the Spiegelman Brothers' table. He was climbing onto a stool as he made his inquiry.

"Who got killed?" asked the bartender.

Leroy plucked the picture out of the bartender's hand, then studied it. "Sure, she was here Wednesday or Thursday. Hold on a mo." Keeping tight hold of the picture, he carried it over to the others. "Remember this dame?"

"Nervous broad," said Edwin, nodding as he tapped Marsha's face with his forefinger. "Sat by herself at that table next to the jukebox."

Jane and I had followed Leroy. She sat in the spare chair; I put my hand on its back. "Which night was this?" I asked them.

Mort was studying the picture now. "It must've been Thursday, pal, because Wednesday I went ice skating and I wasn't here."

"Thursday, yeah," agreed Leroy. "She came in right after

you got into that fight with the sailors about their playing 'Jeepers Creepers' eleven times nonstop on the juke."

"Thirteen times," corrected Mort.

I asked, "What time did she come in?"

Edwin answered, "Little after ten."

"And she was alone?"

Leroy said, "Until the cowboy got here."

"Somebody met her?"

"This dame was alone, but she kept looking at her watch," Mort told me. "The way you do when you're expecting somebody to show up. About ten minutes after she arrived, the cowboy showed up."

"Cowboy how? An actor?"

"Drugstore cowboy," said Leroy, nose wrinkling. "Maybe does extra work in Gene Autry movies. He was wearing Levi's, a checked work shirt, and a leather jacket. Had a new pair of boots and a tan low-crown Stetson, dirty-blond hair. Hat was new, too."

"You ever see him before?" Jane asked them.

"Nope," said Leroy. "Not here and not at the studios."

I said, "Did it look like the girl knew this cowboy?"

Leroy said, "She was meeting the bastard for a drink, wasn't she?"

"Maybe it was a blind date," I said. "When he first walked in, did she seem to recognize him?"

Mort said, "Here's what I think, buddy. No, she didn't know him before, but he'd told her something like he'd be dressed as a Gower Gulch cowpoke. So she recognized him that way, see?"

"And did he recognize her?"

"That wasn't too tough to do, since she was the only good-looking young skirt in the joint alone that night."

Jane asked, "So was it a date?"

All three of the brothers shook their heads. Edwin said, "The cowboy sat with her maybe fifteen, twenty minutes. They had a very serious, very *sotto voce* conversation."

Leroy added, "Then he gets up, bids her a very chilly adios, and ambles out in his new boots. The guy didn't look any too happy."

"How'd she look?" I asked.

"Pleased with herself."

"Like maybe there'd been some kind of business deal negotiated?"

Leroy shrugged his narrow shoulders. "Maybe, but it wasn't movie business, I don't believe," he said finally. "And she wasn't a hooker either."

"The cowboy didn't threaten her?"

"Nope, he just wasn't very cordial."

"How long did she stay after he left?"

"Around ten more minutes, something like that."

I said, "How much drinking was done?"

Mort said, "She had one shot of bourbon with water on the side. The Lone Ranger had a beer. So neither one of them left here drunk, if that's what you want to know."

"Could he have stayed outside, waiting until she came out?"

"Hard to tell, buster," said Leroy. "We lost interest once he walked out of here. You figure it wasn't an accident that killed that girl?"

"I'm keeping an open mind," I told him.

Eighteen

It wasn't until he'd turned off Roxbury Drive in Beverly Hills and gone slouching onto the side street leading to the Britannia Club that Groucho, as he later told me, realized that he was going to have to run a gantlet of tourists.

A party of about fifteen of them, middle-aged and of both sexes, was scattered along both sides of the narrow street. They were peering into shop windows, watching the awning-covered entrance of a currently fashionable little French restaurant known to be frequented by movie stars, snapping pictures, and alert for passing celebrities. Down at the far end of the block a small tour bus was parked.

A thin woman in a fur-trimmed cloth coat assaulted him first. Thrusting a thick blue autograph album at him, she asked, "Can you write your name?"

He clattered to a stop. "Ah, I knew that sooner or later they'd catch up with me and I'd have to pass a literacy test," he said, sadly accepting the book. "And in Hollywood of all places, the mecca for illiterates the world over. I'm not sure whether to sing a snappy chorus of *Mecca Whoopee* or quote from H. L. Mecca's *American Mercury*. All I know is that we always use American mercury in all our thermometers because it's so much nicer than that foreign stuff." Scribbling his name, he returned the album and moved on.

Groucho managed to cover only another ten feet when a heavyset man in a brown double-breasted suit and polka-dot bow tie stepped into his path. "I know who you are," he announced.

"Sorry, that contest ended last week," Groucho informed him, "and we're no longer giving away prizes to people who identify me on the street. We are, however, handing out trophies for the Silliest Ties West of the Pecos and you're definitely going to be in the running for that."

Dodging the man, Groucho resumed his journey.

He was next assailed by a short blond woman who laughed, looked him up and down, and said, "You've got to be Groucho Marx."

"Oh, no, I don't. You're not going to pin that rap on me," he assured her. "I have no less than six reliable witnesses who're prepared to swear that I am actually Anne of Green Gables. Plus, I might add, five pretty irresponsible witnesses, who're ready to claim I'm Anne of Green Bagels."

By the time the woman had located her autograph book in the depths of her purse, Groucho had made his way to the steps of the Britannia.

There a lanky man in a sharkskin suit detained him. "I have a picture of you," the man said, starting to search in his coat pockets.

"They tell me there are now safe and painless ways to remove tattoos."

"It's not a tattoo, it's a photograph."

"That's an unusual thing to have stuck to your backside."

142

"It's not stuck to my backside."

Groucho started to climb the marble steps. "Well, don't come crying to me because your glue isn't working."

"It's in a little album of movie star pictures and I'd really appreciate it if you'd sign it." He found the small book and handed it, open to the right page, over to Groucho.

He scowled at the small photograph. "You're sure this isn't Balzac's death mask?"

"It's you, Mr. Marx. I sent MGM two bits for it."

After signing his name across the small studio portrait, he plucked a dime out of his jacket pocket, and gave it to the lanky man. "They definitely overcharged you, my boy," he said, and went hurrying up into the Britannia Club.

The heavy oaken door of the two-story brownstone building swung open inward while Groucho was still three steps from it.

P. G. Wodehouse emerged, recognized Groucho, and smiled. "Delightful running into you, Marx," he said, extending his hand.

Shaking hands, Groucho smiled up at the tall, balding author. "Delightful running into *you*, Plum."

Wodehouse bestowed what might have been a sympathetic look on him and continued on his way down to the sidewalk.

A profound silence, scented with furniture polish, closed in around Groucho as soon as he entered the lobby of the Britannia Club.

The walls were paneled in dark wood and over the arched entryway to the silent Reading Room hung an oil painting of King George VI. On the left loomed a shadowy cloakroom and on the right a small office that had *Club Secretary* engraved in gold on its pebbled glass upper portion.

Soundlessly the door now eased open.

A slim, pale man, dapper in a navy blue blazer and gray flannel trousers, came floating out. His pale blond hair was parted in the middle and his wrinkle-rimmed eyes were narrowed. "Surely, old man, you've intruded here by mistake?" he suggested in a subdued voice.

"You're the gink who sent for the exterminator, aren't you?" inquired Groucho loudly. "Just let me at those cockroaches."

The club secretary's eyes narrowed even further and he made a hush-hush gesture with his pale right hand. "You have, as I suspected from the outset, blundered onto the wrong premises, my good man," he informed him. "We haven't so much as seen a single insect here at the Britannia ever."

Reaching into a side pocket, Groucho offered, "Would you like to take a gander at some? I brought along samples of cockroaches, termites, mealy bugs, and some strange-looking little green devils that nobody at the office has, thus far, been able to identify."

"No, please, I'm afraid I must ask you to leave."

"Before you do, would you let Randell McGowan know I'm here to keep my appointment with him."

The pale man fingered the gilded club crest on the pocket of his blazer. "You've been jesting with me?"

Groucho rolled his eyes in an apologetic way. "I fear so, yes."

"I must tell you, my dear sir, that I don't especially enjoy having my leg pulled."

"If I had little bitty runty legs like yours, I wouldn't enjoy

144

it either," sympathized Groucho. "Now how's about telling McGowan I'm here?"

The club secretary took a backward step. "Who shall I say wishes to see him?"

"Groucho Marx."

"Groucho?" His eyes narrowed until he appeared to be squinting. "Your given name is Groucho?"

Groucho sighed. "Alas, yes," he admitted. "I was named after a rich uncle in the hopes of a substantial inheritance. But when the old bird kicked off, he left all his dough to a home for oversexed canaries."

"I'll summon someone to escort you to the dining room, which is, I believe, where you'll find Mr. McGowan." He returned, with alacrity, to his office and shut the door.

Approximately five minutes later a reedy, slow-moving man in his early seventies came shuffling in from the Reading Room. He was clad in a venerable suit of tails and held a small sheet of cream-colored paper clutched in his bony right hand. When he'd tottered his way to about three feet of Groucho, he halted and inquired in a polite dim voice, "Mr. Marcus?"

"Close enough."

"If you'd follow me, sir?"

"Darn, I was hoping you were going to say, 'Walk this way.'"

"Beg pardon, sir?"

"And well you should. Lead on."

Perplexity briefly touched the waiter's time-lined face. Then with a resigned sigh, he turned and began slowly to retrace his steps.

The Reading Room contained nine fat dark leather armchairs and a claw-footed table that held a neatly arranged assortment of British periodicals, including *The Illustrated London News* and *The Strand*. On the walls hung several large oil paintings of past Britannia Club cricket teams. Groucho recognized David Niven, C. Aubrey Smith, and Nigel Bruce in two of the paintings.

Sitting in one of the armchairs was C. Aubrey Smith himself. The stately old actor was asleep, snoring sedately, with an open copy of the *London Times* draped across his lap.

There were two other gentlemen occupying the quiet room, but Groucho didn't recognize either. Both looked up from their magazines to scowl at his footfalls coming across the thick Persian carpet.

The shuffling waiter opened a heavy door, then stood aside and whispered, "You'll find Mr. McGowan at table six."

"I appreciate your guiding me here," he said in a whisper. "If I need any help finding my way out, I'll just give a holler."

"Oh, no, sir, you mustn't do that."

Bowing slightly, Groucho slouched into the beam-ceilinged room.

It contained exactly a dozen small tables, each covered with a crisp white linen cloth. At the moment only four of the tables were occupied. There was a small bar in one corner and three other members of the Britannia sat there, quietly drinking.

McGowan was a portly man in his middle forties. He was dressed in a tweedy suit and his black mustache was clipped in military fashion. "Deucedly glad you could find the time to drop by, Groucho, old man."

Groucho sat opposite him. "I didn't know you talked this way in real life."

The actor blinked. "Afraid so, old boy," he said. "Gotten to be a beastly habit. Due to playing far too many pompous sons of Albion since I arrived in Hollywood. Pity, don't you know, but there it is, eh?"

"Both my offspring thought you were splendid in *The Many Loves of Bonny Prince Charlie*," Groucho told him. "It isn't every man who can bring off wearing kilts in Technicolor."

"You're a deucedly perplexing chap, Groucho, old man," said McGowan, picking up his glass and taking a small sip. "Difficult to tell when you're ragging a fellow and when you're sincere."

"Here's the key to deciphering my dialogue," he offered. "I'm never sincere."

"Care for a splash of something, old cock? Having a gin and it myself."

Groucho shook his head. "No, thanks, McGowan," he said, resting both elbows on the table. "Is *The Valley of Fear* going to continue?"

"Afraid so, yes," he said after another sip of his martini. "Mammoth's bringing in Frederick Bauer to take over the direction and we're going back into production next week."

"You're not overjoyed at the prospect?"

The portly actor said, "Getting bloody tired of working with Miles Ravenshaw, if you must know, old fellow. Blighter possesses an enormous ego, even for an actor, and hasn't enough talent to work in the chorus of a Christmas pantomime, let alone the cinema. He makes a dreadful Holmes."

"I hear Twentieth is thinking of doing a Holmes movie with Basil Rathbone."

McGowan winced. "Have you ever been invited to one of those ostentatious parties that Rathbone and his memsahib throw?"

"Once or twice, yes."

"Far too showy for my taste, don't you know. They're definitely, one must say, not British sort of parties."

"You had something to tell me?"

"Well, yes, old boy, although I'm not at all certain it'll help you determine who killed Felix Denker," he said. "There was another dreadful chap, by the way." He picked up his glass once again.

"You have some information about who might've killed Denker?"

"Actually, Groucho, old fellow, I simply overheard a small portion of a conversation a few days ago at the studio," the actor explained. "Wouldn't want this to get around, but there's a young lady playing a small part in the film that I've rather taken a fancy to, don't you know. I was flitting off to meet her on the sly at one of the indoor sets for our picture, one that wasn't being used that day. While making my way there, I chanced to hear some noise coming from the London pub set. Keeping in the shadows, I eavesdropped."

"Eavesdropped on who?"

"Coming to that, dear chap," said McGowan. "It was Erika Klein, Denker's wife, you know, and that young woman who was killed in an automobile accident just a few days later. Marsha Tederow, I believe the poor lass's name was."

"That's her name, yes. She and Erika were arguing?"

"Erika slapped the girl across the face and called her a greedy, conniving bitch. The Tederow girl simply laughed at her, pushed her aside, and left," said the movie Dr. Watson. "I didn't hear anything else of their discussion. The reason this incident struck me as odd is this, Groucho, old boy. Quite a few of us were aware that Denker was apparently having a romance with this Tederow wench, but the word around the studio was that his wife didn't much care."

"You're saying that she apparently did."

"I'm saying, don't you know, that the lady had a seemingly angry encounter with Marsha Tederow," clarified McGowan. "I'm assuming it had to do with her husband's philandering, but I can't swear to that. Still and all, old fellow, I thought you might be able to use the information in some way. Some way, I say, that will put a spanner in Ravenshaw's works."

Groucho promised, "I'll send for a spanner at once."

Nineteen

The Ivy Hotel in downtown Los Angeles had known better days, but that was almost twenty years earlier. Now the sylvan murals that decorated the large lobby's walls were faded and peeling, several of the frolicking shepherdesses looked to have complexion problems, and the gamboling lambs were suffering from mildew. The imitation marble pillars, all eight of them, were chipped and stained, and the one nearest the elevator cages had a distinct list to the left.

Someone had been burning a pungent, churchly incense in the lobby the afternoon I dropped in to call on my old *L.A. Times* informant. The scent didn't mix well with the longer-running smells of disinfectant, fly spray, and unwashed clothes.

A scruffy bulldog was dancing a jig on a threadbare stretch of carpeting in the center of the big domed room. A gaunt man in an oversize tan overcoat was sitting on the gilded sofa near him and keeping time on a sprung tambourine.

"C'mon, Boswell," he urged, "strut your stuff."

The old dog looked weary and forlorn, but he kept spinning and hopping on his shaky hind legs, panting.

The audience for the performance consisted of a small gray-haired woman in a flowered dress and the curly-haired clerk.

On my way to the desk, I stopped near the struggling bulldog. Pointing a thumb down at him, I asked the man with the tambourine, "If I give you a half a buck, will you let him stop?"

"Make it a buck and I'll also buy Boswell a soup bone to gnaw on."

"Deal." I tossed him a silver dollar.

"Take a break, Boswell."

The dog, producing a collapsing accordion sound, slumped down onto the floor.

I continued on to the desk.

"Surely you don't intend to register?" inquired the platinum-haired clerk.

"I'd like to see Tim O'Hearn."

"Well, that must make you just about the only person so inclined in all of Greater Los Angeles." He was using a cologne that smelled strongly of lilacs.

"Which room?"

"Three-thirteen. Elevators are on the blink today, so you'll have to hoof it."

"You ought to spray the lobby with whatever it is you're using on yourself," I advised him, and headed for the imitation-marble staircase.

"My, aren't we catty this afternoon."

All but one of the orange-tinted light bulbs in the dangling fixtures in the third-floor hallway were burned out and the survivor was flickering badly.

Behind the door of 313 a radio was playing loudly. I recognized the voice of Harry Whitechurch, who'd been the announcer on our late *Groucho Marx, Private Eye* radio show, booming above the organ music. "Once again," he was saying, "it's time for *The Struggle for Happiness*, the heartwarming story of one student nurse's search for love and a satisfying career in our troubled modern world. Our show is brought to you by Bascom's foamy shampoo, the purest . . ."

I knocked on the door. "Tim, it's me."

The radio stopped.

"Who?" asked Tim O'Hearn, not opening the door.

"Frank Denby."

"You sound like him."

"Lots of people have been telling me that of late. Can it be because I am Frank Denby? C'mon, Tim, let me in."

The door opened a few inches and O'Hearn, a thin, worn-out man of fifty, looked out at me. "I can't be too careful."

"Apparently not."

After a few seconds he moved back from the doorway. "You might as well come in, Frank."

All the shades were down and the venerable dark brown drapes drawn in the small room. "You've given up cheese sandwiches."

"A doctor I bumped into in Pershing Square a few weeks back told me cheese was bad for me." Sitting on the edge of his unmade folding bed, he nodded me toward an armchair. "Make yourself comfortable."

I gingerly lifted a saucer that held the remains of a moldering sandwich off the seat and sat. "And what is it you've switched to?"

"Baloney—it's a better source of protein."

Part of another baloney sandwich, rich with some sort of green mold, was perched atop a scattered pile of old, much-annotated racing forms near the lopsided bureau.

"So what have you found out about—"

153

"I ought to get more than five bucks for this particular assignment, Frank," my informant complained. "No, I ought to get hazard pay as well."

"All I asked you for was a line on locating Franz Henkel."

Hunching his shoulders, O'Hearn glanced at the masked windows. "Usually you're curious about gangsters and thugs, and that's dangerous enough," he said. "But now I'm brushing shoulders with Nazis and Gestapo agents and—"

"Wait, whoa. How's Henkel connected with the Gestapo?"

"I'm not sure he is," admitted O'Hearn. "But the guy is in the Bund and groups like that. It makes me really uneasy."

"Any idea where he's hiding out?"

O'Hearn's lean face took on a pained expression and he rubbed a knuckle under his nose. "I don't know for sure yet, but I got you a lead on a guy who does. Thing is, you're going to have to deal directly with this bastard."

"Who is he?"

"Name is Lionel Von Esh," answered my informant. "He works as some kind of stagehand out at the Mammoth studios. Word is he's not an especial pal of this Henkel's, but he knows where the guy is lying low and he's willing to sell that info."

"Okay, where do I contact this Von Esh?"

"He frequents a place in Hollywood called Siegfried's Rathskeller. It's just off Cherokee and sounds like it must be a German hangout."

"It does at that. Is he expected there tonight?"

O'Hearn nodded. "Any time after ten," he said. "And he wants twenty bucks for what he knows."

"You contacted him directly?"

"Naw, but the guy who set this up is reliable, Frank. Trust me."

154

I stood up and took out my wallet. "How do I recognize Von Esh?" "He's got reddish blond hair that he wears in one of those heinie haircuts. And he has an X-shaped scar just under his left eye." He traced an *X* under his eye and then held out the hand to me.

I passed him a five-dollar bill. "Keep digging around about the Denker murder, see what you pick up."

"Okay, but if storm troopers bust in here and rough me up, just remember how little you paid me."

"If they kill you, though," I said, "I've got a swell wreath we can use."

At 4:00 P.M., carrying a dozen red roses wrapped in green paper, I walked confidently in to the sunny reception room of the Golden Hills Rest Home out in the Valley. It had taken three phone calls to former newspaper colleagues to obtain this particular address. I went striding right up to the desk, where a plump woman in a pale green nurse's uniform sat with hands folded and a smile on her face.

"Didn't it turn out to be a lovely day?" she asked me.

"It certainly did," I agreed, returning her smile.

"And how can we help you here at Golden Hills?"

Holding the bouquet of roses a little forward, I said, "I'm Albert Payson Terhune, chairman of the Shut-in Visitor Committee of the Screen Writers Guild."

"My, that sounds like a fascinating occupation."

"It is. We've just learned that one of our members, Clair Rickson, is residing here under the name Clarinda Raffles," I explained, rattling the flowers. "I've dropped by to deliver what we like to call a Sunshine Shower and present her with—"

"Oh, what a shame," said the jovial nurse. "That old toss-pot checked out at noon and left with a disreputable-looking buffoon who appeared to be three sheets to the wind himself. What paper are you with?"

"I'm not a newspaperman," I assured her. "She really left?"

"This is a voluntary sanitarium," the nurse said. "We can't keep anybody here against their will. You newspaper guys aren't too efficient, if you ask me. You're the third one who's dropped by since she left us." She leaned a plump elbow on the desktop. "I must admit, though, that your spiel was the nearest to convincing. But I'd get a better fake name, since, like me, a lot of people probably read Terhune's dog stories when they were tots."

"How's Richard Harding Davis?"

She shook her head. "Lot of people read him, too."

"Frank Denby?"

"That's good," she said. "Has that nice ring of nonentity to it. Use that one."

I asked, "Any idea who it was Clair Rickson left with?"

"He claimed he was Roger Connington."

Connington was a third-rate screenwriter who worked now and then over at Mammoth. "Was he going to deliver her to her own home?"

"From what I overheard, I'd say she was going to shack up with him for a spell."

I eased one rose out of the bunch and presented it to her. "Thanks for the help."

"Who's going to get the rest of the roses?"

"Thought I'd give them to my wife."

"That's very nice." She placed her rose on her blotter.

Turning, I walked away.

156

Twenty

Zanzibar the Astounding did look quite a bit like Edmund Lowe. He parted his hair in the middle like the actor, his waxed mustache was similar. The only thing that spoiled the overall illusion was the fact that he was only five foot one.

After he shook hands with me, Nan warned him, "No nickels out of his nose, Larry."

The magician, who'd been reaching toward my nose, lowered his hand. "Sorry, honey," he said.

"He's compulsive about doing tricks," Groucho's secretary explained to me.

Zanzibar caused six or seven brand-new nickels to come cascading out of his own nose to clink into his palm. "Nan is more understanding than most," he said, closing his hand over the coins and jingling them.

It was a few minutes shy of 6:00 P.M. and I'd dropped by the office for a meeting with Groucho. He was, Nan had informed me, across the street visiting Moonbaum's delicatessen and was expected to return momentarily.

"I've got some bad news for you and Groucho," Nan said

after I seated myself in one of the rattan chairs against the wall of the office.

Groucho kept an unusual selection of magazines in the rack and I set aside the copy of *Ranch Romances* I'd just picked up to ask her, "Bad news about what?"

"Your competition with Miles Ravenshaw," she answered. "Tell him, Larry."

Swallowing the cigarette he'd just lit, Zanzibar said, "Ravenshaw and his wife are throwing a big Christmas party this Saturday night at their place in Brentwood. I'm one of the three magicians they've hired to roam around and entertain their guests." Absently, he began plucking colored eggs out of the armpit of his suit coat. When he had five of them, he started juggling.

"Get to the point," Nan reminded him, frowning.

Zanzibar tossed all five eggs toward the office ceiling and then clapped his hands. The eggs vanished. "The word is," he resumed, "that Ravenshaw plans to announce the solution to the Felix Denker murder at the party."

I assumed a skeptical expression. "Publicity stunt," I said. "He hasn't solved a damn thing."

"It could be," suggested Nan, "that that hambone really has come up with a solution."

I asked the magician, "Any details of what he plans to announce?"

"Nope, I've told you all I heard." He sneezed, then started pulling brightly colored silk handkerchiefs out of his breast pocket.

"I knew Houdini would eventually come up with a way to communicate with us from beyond the grave," said Groucho as he came bounding in with his paper bag from the deli. "Signal flags, of course."

"Groucho, this is Larry Zansky, also known as the Astounding Zanzibar," said his secretary.

"Pleased to meet you, Mr. Marx."

Placing his free hand on the magician's shoulder, Groucho said, "Whatever you do, my boy, I want you to promise me you'll never saw this woman in half."

Twilight was closing in outside as Groucho walked over to the marble-topped café table he kept in one corner of his private office. Slumping into one of the cane-bottom chairs, he uncapped the thermos he'd fetched back from Moonbaum's. "You're absolutely certain, Rollo, you don't want any borscht?" he inquired while he poured purplish soup into his Shirley Temple cereal bowl.

"Absolutely, yes." I was perched on the edge of his desk and facing him.

Groucho lifted a matzo cracker out of the open box sitting on the table. "Did you know that borscht contains all the essential vitamins and minerals—plus, according to an erudite article in the latest edition of *The Lancet*, several other vitamins that won't do you a damn bit of good whatsoever?"

He was breaking the cracker into crackly bits when the phone on his desk rang.

I picked up the handset and held it out to him.

Bouncing up, he took the phone. "Hollywood Crematorium and Columbarium," he answered. "What do you mean it lacks dignity, Zeppo? What's more dignified than an undertaking establishment? But surely you didn't invest in a telephone call merely to chastise me for my girlish tomfoolery and . . . You did? That's splendid. Hold on, I'll take notes."

I handed him a yellow legal pad and his fountain pen.

Groucho put the pad across his knees: "Proceed, Zep. . . . Golly, can such things be? No, I'm not doubting your word nor the veracity of your London sources. . . . Give me the name of the store again. Bland's Book Emporium on Museum Street. A clerk, you say, until he was suspected of dipping in the till . . . Toured with whose provincial company? Hannibal Swineford? That must've looked enticing up in lights. . . . Next a chorus boy in West End musicals, followed by bit parts in the British cinema. Also a brief stint in Berlin in the early 1930s? But never so much as set foot in Scotland Yard? Yes, I know that's what you've been telling me, brother dear, but I like to sum up things in my well-known pithy fashion. . . . No, I haven't developed a lisp. What about . . . All right, I know you're a busy fellow, Zeppo. Just living down the disgrace of putting your brothers in a fiasco like *Room Service* sounds like a full-time occupation to me and then you've . . . No, seriously, I am eternally grateful. Not to mention internally grateful and infernally grapefruit. And I live for the day, however distant, when I can return the favor. Good night, sweet prince."

"So Miles Ravenshaw's an even bigger phony that we thought?"

"I asked Zeppo to check with some of his theatrical cronies over in Great Britain about Ravenshaw's background." He nodded at the phone. "He just reported his findings. That hambone never set foot in Scotland Yard, he never even strolled by the joint on his way to work as an absconding bookshop clerk." He set the pad on his desk, returning to his soup.

"We ought to make this news known to the public," I suggested, "in the most interesting way possible."

Groucho snapped a cracker in half above his borscht. "What better setting for our exposé than Ravenshaw's Christmas festivities this Saturday night, Rollo?" he said, brightening. "We'll have the Astounding Sani-Flush smuggle us in as mystic assistants and, just before the ham of hams rises up to offer his erroneous solution to the murder case, we'll unmask and reveal Ravenshaw as the four-flusher he is. It will be a dramatic moment equal to Eliza crossing the ice or Ted Healy poking all three of his Stooges in the eye simultaneously."

I was leaning against the office wall next to the eagle-topped brass coat tree that held a raccoon overcoat, a paisley shawl, a faded fez, and one of Groucho's Captain Spaulding pith helmets. "Ravenshaw might be able to top us, though," I pointed out. "If he does announce the name of the killer and he happens to be absolutely right."

"He won't be right."

"But just suppose he is."

Groucho ingested three spoonfuls of borscht, thoughtfully. "Then we'll simply have to offer our solution to the case immediately after we expose him as a poltroon," he concluded. "Or maybe we ought to expose him as a macaroon, which might go over better with the crowd."

"I hope you won't write me off as a hopeless pessimist, Groucho," I mentioned, "but I see one possible snag in this plan."

"Yes, so do I, Little Lulu," he conceded. "We don't yet have a crystal-clear idea of who the murderer is."

"Bingo," I said. "That's the same flaw I spotted."

Standing, Groucho pointed a finger toward the ceiling.

"What we have to do immediately, if not sooner, is compare notes on all that we've learned in our separate investigations today," he said. "That may well put us close to the solution."

"Why didn't I think of that?" I said.

Twenty-one

The framed poster on the office wall was for *A Night at the Opera*. Groucho was standing with his back to it, rubbing his hands together and making a gratified chuckling noise. "We've got it, Rollo," he told me, "I do believe we've worked out a very plausible solution to the whole mess."

I'd been sitting at his desk, making notes in the legal pad. "Sounds like it, yeah," I agreed. "Though we're still pretty short on proof, Groucho."

"Okay, let's go over this once more and see if mayhap we can fill in some more blanks." He held up his left hand and started ticking off fingers. "Firstly, using the finger of the first part, Marsha Tederow decided to give blackmail a try. That was the precipitating factor, the knocked-down domino that started the rest of them to tumbling over." He moved away from the wall and commenced pacing in a fuzzy circle. "She'd learned something about somebody and figured she could cash in on it. And what did she find out?"

"Something to do with Dr. Helga Krieger," I said without consulting our notes. "We're assuming that back in the early 1930s somebody fairly high up in Nazi circles determined that

Dr. Krieger ought to come to the United States, probably to stand by for spy and espionage work. Only problem was that, loyal Hitler supporter that she was, she was also well known as a Nazi. So she lost some weight, had her features altered, and assumed an entirely new identity. The dodge worked and she got safely settled in Los Angeles. Nobody suspected who she really was and she just had to wait around until her bosses in Germany contacted her."

"And how did Marsha tumble to the masquerade? Where'd she get those books by the good doctor?"

"Obviously from somebody who knew about the switch."

"We know that Felix Denker became suddenly solvent at about the same time that Dr. Krieger dropped out of sight in the dear old Fatherland," picked up Groucho, his knees bent a bit more. "It seems probable, therefore, that he was approached by somebody affiliated with the Nazi party and offered a deal. You help us smuggle the new, improved Dr. Krieger into America, Felix, old bean, and we'll see that all your gambling debts are settled and you get a few bucks extra to boot."

"Which would mean he probably wasn't as much of an anti-fascist as he pretended."

"Hell, maybe the guy wasn't even as Jewish as he pretended," observed Groucho. "All right, he marries a lady who's supposedly a respected historian named Erika Klein and they migrate to the Golden West. Erika might really be Erika, but it's more likely that she's really Helga after a very profound nose job."

"That's something we can't prove at the moment," I said. "But it fits what we think must've happened. Denker, who's never much liked his fictitious wife, starts to fool around. And,

164

when he eventually gets involved with Marsha, he lets slip to her that his whole marriage is something cooked up by the Nazis for espionage purposes."

"He shows her the books by Dr. Helga that he's had stowed in the attic. He maybe even suggests that the FBI might be able to use the picture of the original face to compare with Erika's new puss and prove scientifically it was the same lady."

"Marsha turns out to be even more mercenary than Denker realized. She sees a way to make quite a bit of extra money," I said. "If Erika is an important planted German agent, then there must be people with considerable money behind her. Her bosses in Berlin wouldn't want her exposed, they wouldn't want anybody even to hint that Erika wasn't what she seemed. Marsha approaches Erika and says she'll go to the FBI unless she's paid off on a regular basis."

"The first time she approaches Erika with her proposition, Erika loses her temper, calls Marsha names, and belts her one," said Groucho. "That's what Dr. Watson overheard part of while pussyfooting around backstage."

"Then Erika figures she has to do something to keep Marsha quiet. She'll con her into thinking she's going to pay off. That explains the phone call inviting her to the meeting at the Cutting Room with the cowboy."

"The cowpoke seemingly agrees to Marsha's terms, says she'll get her first payoff sometime tomorrow, and goes ambling off. But he waits outside, follows Marsha, and forces her car off the road," says Groucho. "Maybe he slips downhill into that gully to make sure she doesn't get out of the burning car."

"I did finally get a look at a copy of the accident report," I said. "Initially the police didn't find anything suspicious."

"They may if they go over the stuff again, because the cowboy has to be the one responsible for the girl's death."

"And who is he?"

"Another Nazi agent, somebody Erika rounded up for the job."

I tapped my eraser on the legal pad. "I wonder if Marsha had ever met this guy Gunther."

Groucho frowned, thinking. "Yeah, if she'd never seen the lad, he could have simply donned a wig and Western togs and played the part of the go-between."

I said, "Okay, when Denker hears that Marsha's been killed, he realizes what's happened. He broods about it, tries to work up enough nerve to at least confide in his old buddy Professor Hoffman."

"But then he gets to thinking that if he turns Erika in, he's not going to look too good with the authorities himself," said Groucho. "Finally, though, by Monday he decides to have a showdown with Erika. He'll accuse her of having his lover killed and tell her, come what may, he's going to turn her over to the law."

"They arrange an out of the way meeting on Soundstage Two in the Two-twenty-one-B set. But instead of agreeing to turn herself in, Erika shoots Denker—maybe with his own gun—and leaves him sitting in Sherlock Holmes's favorite chair."

"And that's why Denker was trying to scrawl a swastika as he was dying. To point to a hidden Nazi." Groucho frowned. "The only problem with all this is the fact that Erika officially signed out of Mammoth a good two hours or more before Denker was shot."

"Mammoth isn't Devil's Island or Alcatraz," I reminded. "She could've sneaked back in for their rendezvous."

He nodded. "It makes sense, the whole scenario, Rollo. But, as you so wisely pointed out, we sure as hell don't have much in the way of proof."

Getting up, I started pacing in his wake. "Suppose we can find Franz Henkel?" I suggested. "We turn him over to the cops and establish that he positively didn't kill Denker. That would convince Sergeant Norment to take a look at Erika and our theories about—"

"Very well, we'll nab Henkel," agreed Groucho. "I'll pick you up at your seaside villa about nine-thirty and we'll slip into Siegfried's Rathskeller looking guileless and for all the world like Hans and Fritz Katzenjammer. I'll even wear my goy necktie and . . . the letters!"

"Huh?"

"Who really wrote those threatening letters dear Erika gave me copies of?" He sprinted to his desk, yanked open a drawer, and grabbed out a manila folder. "If Henkel isn't the killer, then maybe he didn't write these letters either. If they're faked, experts can determine who really—"

"Could be Erika penned them herself," I suggested. "Let me show them to Jane. She's very good at spotting lettering and handwriting styles. It won't be official, but it—"

"Good, rush them to your missus. Tomorrow at the funeral, I'll contrive to swipe a sample of the dear widow's handwriting," Groucho volunteered. "And, while I'm at it, I'll gather up all the spare change that's slipped under the seats in the hearse."

The moment I turned onto our driveway, the front door of the house flapped open and Jane came running out.

I hit the brakes, turned off the engine, and jumped from the car. "What is it—what's wrong?"

She was wearing a short yellow terry cloth robe and was barefoot. "Are you okay? You're all right?" she asked, running across the lawn to put her arms, tight, around me.

"Far as I know, yep." I hugged her with considerable enthusiasm. "Were you expecting otherwise?"

Jane started to laugh, then stopped and hugged me again. "I guess I got carried away," she said. "After reading that note they left."

"Okay, easy now," I told my wife. "Let's go inside first, okay?"

"I called Groucho's office as soon as I read it, but his answering service girl told me everybody'd just left for the day."

I put my arm around her shoulders, guided her along the path to the lighted doorway. "You aren't wearing much," I mentioned.

"I'd just come out of the shower, when I heard a noise on the porch," Jane explained as we crossed the threshold. "I saw a folded note being slipped under the door."

"I'm hoping you didn't open the damned door."

"I didn't, but I looked out through the venetian blinds," she said. "No sign of anybody or a car."

"Well, thus far nobody's tried to kill me." I noticed a sheet of paper lying on the coffee table. "That the note?" I let go of her to walk over to the table.

Jane nodded, took a couple of slow openmouthed breaths in and out. "Go ahead and read it," she said.

It was hand-lettered and said: "Frank Denby, you'll die if you don't mind your own business. So will your Jew friend."

"Groucho would say this is a good sign. Shows we've got them scared."

"And they've got me scared," she said.

I put the letter back on the table, weighted it down with one of the little crystal cats Jane's aunt in Fresno persisted in sending us. "Sit down on the sofa, take a few more deep breaths," I advised my wife. "I want to get something from the car to show you."

"You think I got hysterical, huh?"

"I'm flattered that there's at least one person in the world who's that concerned about me."

"I was the same way when you had the flu last August."

"At least influenza doesn't slide nasty warnings under your door. Although that might be helpful in getting ready for it." I ran out to where I'd abandoned my Ford and retrieved the folder I'd borrowed from Groucho.

"What's that stuff?" she asked.

"These are threatening notes allegedly sent to Felix Denker and to Erika Klein." I spread them out next to my threat. "Same lettering, isn't it?"

Hugging herself, Jane bent forward to compare the three letters. "Yeah, I'd say so, Frank. Who sent these others?"

"Erika Klein claims it was the murderous gaffer Franz Henkel."

"No, nope, not at all," she said, shaking her head. "A woman wrote these."

"You can tell with lettering whether a woman did it?"

"Hey, lettering is part of my profession," she reminded me. "I've studied it since I was a little kid. This was done by a lady who was trying to look tough."

"That would tie in with our theory," I said, sitting down close beside her. "You smell like wildflowers."

"Darn, you're the ninth man who's mentioned that so far today."

I grinned. "I notice your wiseass side is emerging. Meaning you're calming down."

"Gallows humor," she suggested. "Explain your theory to me, huh?"

I gave her a fairly detailed account of what Groucho and I had come up with. Concluding by saying, "We were going to go to a German hangout over in Hollywood to try to contact a lout who's supposed to know where Franz Henkel is hiding out. But if there are people lurking around here, I don't want to leave you alone or—"

"Here's a simple solution, then: I'll tag along with you."

"You wouldn't want to come to Siegfried's Rathskeller."

"Sounds like fun," she said. "They might have an oompah band and we could dance. You hardly ever take me out dancing now that we're married."

"I'm a little rusty on the steps of the Rhinelander," I told her, sighing in a way that signaled defeat. "But, okay, you can come along. But two things you have to do."

Jane smiled. "You need but speak. I'm in an extremely compliant mood," she assured me.

"You're going to have to be extremely careful," I said. "And you're going to have to put on some clothes."

Twenty-two

This is a good sign," said Groucho. "It shows that we've got them scared."

Jane winked at me and made that sound you make when you're trying to swallow a laugh.

Groucho was standing, wide-legged, in the middle of our living room with the threatening letter in his hand. He was wearing a somewhat tweedy suit and a hat he claimed was in the Tyrolean style. "Sounds as though you're suffering from a respiratory ailment, my child," he observed as he returned the sheet of paper to me.

"I think I must be allergic to feathers," she said while I helped her get into her coat. "Especially silly feathers like the one you've got sticking in your hat band."

He linked his fingers, pressed both hands over his heart, and rose up on his toes. "Glorioski, this is scrumptious," he exclaimed. "I truly feel that I've finally become part of your family, Rollo. Your lovely wife insults me in the same heartwarming manner as is utilized by my four hulking brothers as well as my present wife and children."

Jane moved closer and hugged him. "I only insult people

I'm fond of," she assured him. "And, really now, that is a dippy-looking hat."

"It's part of my disguise," he explained, easing free of her embrace and seeming somewhat uneasy. "I intend to stroll boldly into this Germanic stronghold this evening looking for all the world like an Austrian brewer on vacation."

"I suppose there must be a few Austrian brewers who wear silly hats," she conceded.

He squared his shoulders and clicked his heels together. "Permission to change the subject, mum," he said. "Frank tells me you've had some insights into who penned our growing collection of threatening missives."

"Well, I'm certain that Franz Henkel didn't produce them," she said.

I went over to the mirror above our fireplace to check my tie.

"You're sure of that?" he asked her.

"The two letters you gave Frank plus the one that was shoved under our door tonight," Jane said, "were all written by a woman. The same woman."

"You can tell the sex of the writer even with block printing?"

"Sure."

He gave a pleased nod. "That means Erika definitely could've done the job."

"It's quite possible, yes."

"It follows, therefore, that Franz Henkel is definitely a red herring or a scapegoat or some other mythical beast," said Groucho. "All the more reason to locate the lout and find out exactly what, if anything, he actually does have to do with this mess."

"This is funny," I said, staring at my image. "I just realized that I, too, look a hell of a lot like an Austrian brewer. We should be able to breeze right into Siegfried's Rathskeller unnoticed."

"Especially since Jane looks like Miss Rheingold." Groucho slouched over and opened the door. "Come along, kiddies, time to be out upon our appointed rounds."

Siegfried's Rathskeller was a large, loud, bright-lit barn of a place, with over fifty tables and at least two hundred patrons crowded inside. On the right side of the high, wide entryway hung a nearly life-size oil painting of Adolf Hitler in one of his majestic führer poses and on the left an equally large portrait of Bismarck. Atop a bandstand at the far end of the restaurant a brass band was playing exuberantly. There were two tubas, two cornets, a bass drum, a huge set of cymbals, and a piccolo. The members of the band, husky fellows all, were red in the face and perspiring from their musical efforts. They wore lederhosen, shorts, embroidered vests, and red hats. The waiters were similarly built and costumed, except that they were hatless, and the barmaids had braided blond hair, low-cut blouses, and bright rustic skirts. The big room was hot and smoky and the predominant smell was that of fried sausage.

At three of the tables against the right wall an assortment of crew-cut men in the tan uniform of the German American Bund were gathered. Most of them were laughing and now and then clanking their beer steins together.

There were also family groups and couples at many of the tables, eating vast meals and drinking beer of varying hues.

"I'm glad I decided not to wear my Star of David in my

lapel tonight," said Groucho close by my ear as our waiter escorted us to a vacant table near the crowded oval dance floor.

After we were seated and alone, Jane said quietly, "This may not be too good an idea, Groucho."

"Nonsense, my child." He picked up his menu and tapped it. "Says right here they only have pogroms on Friday and Saturday nights."

As casually as I could I glanced around at the nearby tables. Nobody seemed to be paying any particular attention to us.

"I suppose it would be a mistake to order gefilte fish," said Groucho.

"Hush," advised my wife, putting her hand, briefly, over his.

"Actually, children, I made a list of things I won't say while we're within these sacred halls," he told us. "No remarks utilizing the word *wurst* in droll ways. Such as 'The wurst is yet to come,' 'Do your wurst,' 'This conversation is going from bad to wurst,' et cetera."

The waiter, who had a fairly thick accent, returned and asked, "May I take your order, gentlemen and lady?"

"Didn't you use to work as Sig Ruman's stand-in?" inquired Groucho.

"Three beers," I said quickly.

"Coming right up." The waiter went away.

Jane inched her chair closer to mine. "I'm feeling a mite scared," she admitted. "That picture of Hitler and those lunkheads with the swastika armbands—and, I don't know, it just feels spooky in here."

"I'm not feeling all that relaxed myself," admitted Groucho. "Have you spotted Von Esh yet, Frank?"

"Keep in mind that I've never seen the guy or even a picture of him," I said. "He's supposed to be thin with short-cropped blond hair and an X-shaped scar under his eye."

"With our luck there'll be a reunion of Heidelberg dueling enthusiasts here tonight, all with X scars."

"Maybe there's another way to do this," said Jane. "Frank, you could contact your friend O'Hearn again and—"

"Hold on," I said, nodding to my right. "At the small table next to the family that's attacking that platter of blood sausage. I think that's him."

Very casually, Groucho glanced in that direction. "Thin, short hair, requisite scar, and he's trying to let on he's not watching us."

"O'Hearn gave him a description of you and me, Groucho."

"That may account for his look of perplexity. He may think I'm actually William Powell and he's wondering why I don't have a mustache. Eventually he'll realize that—"

"Soon as our drinks arrive," I said, "I'll walk over there. I'll sit with him for a few minutes and buy the address we want. You and Jane can stay here."

"That's a nifty idea," said Groucho. "That way we can get what we want without attracting too much attention by all traipsing over there or having him join us here. Shouldn't take more than a few minutes."

"Yeah, I'll—"

From the right of our table a deep, loud voice said, "Groucho Marx, you son of a bitch. You've got a hell of a nerve coming here!"

175

Twenty-three

Jack O'Banyon was a large, wide man. He had a strong jaw and a weather-beaten face, and his broad flat nose had been broken at least twice. He was standing, fists on hips, close to our table and smiling a nasty smile down at Groucho.

O'Banyon specialized in tough soldier-of-fortune parts and if directors couldn't get Victor McLaglen, they got him. His most successful pictures were *Charge of the Khyber Rifles* in 1936 and *Fighting Men of the Foreign Legion* in 1937. Back in 1933 there was talk that he'd get an Oscar nomination for his performance in *Toilers to the Sea*, but that didn't happen. Politically he was what you could call a fascist and a bully and a little over a year ago he'd gathered together some similarly minded actors and movie people to form O'Banyon's Silver Shirt Brigade. They dressed up in specially made uniforms, practiced military drills, and rode horses in mock cavalry exercises.

Tonight the husky actor was wearing his uniform. Silver shirt, black jodhpurs and boots, and a crimson armband that displayed a Maltese cross in a white circle. "Didn't you hear me, Julius?" he asked.

Glancing up at him, Groucho lit a cigar and blew out smoke. "Has your Boy Scout unit been called up for active duty, Jack?"

Still smiling, O'Banyon leaned closer to Groucho. Standing crowded just behind him were three other Silver Shirts.

One of them I recognized as Warren Sawtell, a tough-guy actor who was part of John Ford's circle. He had his right hand pressed tight against his side and was clutching something that looked an awful lot like a blackjack.

"This is my sort of hangout, Groucho, and we don't like to see Hebrews here," said O'Banyon. "It's bad enough you people run the movie business, we sure as hell don't intend to socialize with you."

"Screw the polite conversation," said Sawtell. "Let's just toss him out on his ass."

"Don't be rude, Warren," cautioned O'Banyon, resting his hand on the back of Groucho's chair. "See, this particular Jew is a real believer in democracy and free speech. He gives a lot of his Jew money to the Anti-Nazi League and to the Communists, who oppose a patriot like Franco in Spain. What we have to do, you understand, is try a little free speech on him ourselves, convey to him the idea that he better just leave in a hurry. But, please, no rough stuff. Yet."

"The hell with that," persisted Sawtell, shoving his way closer to our table. "He's got no right to be here. They should never have let him in."

My stomach seemed to be shrinking, I could hear my heart beating in my ears, and my throat had gone sandpaper dry. Swallowing a couple of times, I stood up and turned to Sawtell. "Be a real good idea if you guys just went away and got a table of your own," I told him. "Or maybe you can go and dance with each other. Anyway, do something besides annoying us."

Deep scowl lines grew on the thickset actor's forehead. "You calling me a pansy?"

"Excuse me, I guess those tight pants fooled me. Or maybe it's the wildflower perfume you're wearing."

"Frank," said Jane quietly, reaching up and taking hold of my hand. "What say we simply make a discreet exit?"

Groucho nodded. "She's got a splendid idea, Rollo," he said, starting to rise. "We probably aren't going to be able to conduct our business now anyway."

The only snag in that plan was the fact that Sawtell, growling through clenched teeth, came charging straight at me. It was definitely a blackjack the guy was holding.

"Frank!" said Jane, pushing back in her chair and getting to her feet. The chair teetered, then fell over backwards and smacked the floor.

Fortunately, five years on the police beat taught me something about taking care of myself. I sidestepped the actor's charge, side-armed him, and thrust my foot between his legs.

He went tripping over, slammed into our table.

The table creaked and one of its legs cracked. Sawtell fell to the hardwood floor, smacking it with the right side of his face.

The table collapsed and the ashtray dropped and banged against Sawtell's skull. The tablecloth unfurled and dropped down to shroud him.

I dived and threw three punches at the place where I calculated his chin ought to be. I connected and the actor gave a sighing moan and went slack.

Pressing my palm against the floor, I started to push myself upright.

"Another one!" warned Jane.

I spun in time to see a wide, uniformed Silver Shirt starting to aim a booted foot at my ribs.

"Son of a bitch," he said.

I stumbled slightly, but I managed to dodge the kick.

Kicking at nothing but air put him off balance. Before he could straighten up, Jane had grabbed up her fallen chair and shoved it into him, the way a lion tamer works with his big cats.

The guy yowled, toppled over, and landed hard on his backside next to the unconscious Sawtell.

O'Banyon was reaching into his pocket for something.

Catching hold of his arm, Groucho suggested, "I really think we've all had enough exercise for one day, Jack. If this continues somebody's going to summon the riot squad."

After a few snarling seconds, O'Banyon ordered, "That's enough, men. Leave them alone."

Groucho tipped his Tyrolean hat. "Much obliged."

When O'Banyon smiled this time his lips climbed up to reveal his clenched teeth. "Just get out of here, Hebe, and don't come back," he said, pointing at Groucho.

I moved around and took hold of Jane's arm. "Let's aim for that side exit just over there."

On the floor Sawtell was beginning to groan and thrash some under the cloth.

Jane and I started weaving our way through the tables and the customers of the rathskeller. We were, by this time, attracting considerable attention.

Groucho followed. Every time one of the patrons called an insult or a slur, he smiled amiably and replied, "I'm terribly sorry but we're unable to fulfill any requests for autographs at this time."

I noticed that the guy who might have been Von Esh was no longer at his table.

"The band is getting ready to strike up the 'Horst Wessel Song,' " said Groucho. "And those Bund boys are starting to cast baleful glances in our direction. Let's make haste, Rollo."

Just before we reached the exit our waiter caught up with us. "Sir," he said, "someone wanted you to have this." He slipped me a small folded sheet of pale blue paper.

"Thanks." I took it, dropped it into a pocket, and gave him two quarters.

I got to the door first, shouldered it open. "You first, Jane," I instructed, putting my hand on her back and pushing her out into the foggy night.

Just before Groucho reached the exit a beer bottle came sailing out of the crowd. It hit his hat and knocked it off his head.

"Nobody seems especially fond of that hat," he said, diving through the doorway.

I took two steps after him and then somebody caught hold of my arm and pulled me back.

"Swine, you don't get away that easy."

It was one of the German American Bund members, in full uniform. A lanky guy with spiky blond hair. He was perspiring a lot and his eyes were a bit bleary.

I yanked free of his grip, kneed him in the groin, and ran.

The guy howled, doubled up, and hopped a couple of times.

Outside Jane was starting to come back to see what had become of me. "You okay?"

"Run," I advised, taking hold of her hand.

Groucho was standing a few yards down the sidewalk. When he saw me emerge, he spun and started double-timing toward the place we'd left his Cadillac.

From the doorway of the club somebody shouted, "Stay away, you lousy Hebes!"

I glanced back as we ran. Four or five husky lads were crowding the exit, but nobody was giving chase. I decided against thumbing my nose at them.

"Not the most graceful exit I've ever made," commented Groucho when we caught up with him. "But, I must say, Primo, you were handy with your fists."

"You ought to see the way he works out with his punching bag," said Jane. "He's a regular Joe Palooka."

We reached the car and while Groucho shoved in behind the wheel, I got Jane and myself into the backseat. "This would be a good time to beat a hasty retreat, Groucho."

He started the engine, released the brake, and executed a U-turn. "I have to admit, children, that dropping in on Siegfried's Rathskeller this evening was a tactical error."

"Probably, yeah," I agreed. "My fault as much as yours for thinking we could get in and out without any trouble."

Groucho said, "I didn't expect it would get that rough. Or that O'Banyon would be having a Silver Shirt jamboree on the premises."

Jane put an arm around me, leaning her head against my chest. "You didn't sustain any serious damage, did you?"

"No, I'm fine," I told her. "Thanks for helping out with that chair."

"Saw Clyde Beatty do that in the circus once," she said. "Not with a Nazi but with a lion. The basic steps are the same, though."

From the front seat Groucho asked, "Where do we go from here? Since we never got to have our chat with Von Esh, we—"

"The message," I remembered. I took the note out of my pocket and unfolded it. Reaching up, I clicked on the overhead light.

In neat handwriting the note said: "Too dangerous here. Meet me at the Ebbtide Café, Venice, 11:30 tonight. VE."

Twenty-four

The Ebbtide Café sat alone near a stretch of beach on the outskirts of the town of Venice. Night fog came drifting in, swirling around us as Groucho and I walked across the white gravel of the small parking lot. Unseen foghorns were hooting far off.

"All newlyweds have squabbles," Groucho was pointing out. "My wife and I had such lively ones that the Gillette Razor Company offered to sponsor them on the radio."

"This meeting with Von Esh could turn out to be dangerous, so it makes sense to—"

"It could be dangerous?" He stopped, putting a hand on my arm. "Maybe you should've dropped me off at Jane's old art school chum's house, too."

We resumed walking toward the café, which gave the impression of having been built primarily out of bits of lumber that had washed up on the beach.

Much against her will, I'd left Jane to wait for us at the home of a married girlfriend in Bayside. The fact that I didn't want her risking her life hadn't impressed Jane much.

"She's a very independent woman," I said, pushing open the lopsided door of the little café.

"And quite original and inventive when it comes to derogatory terms to apply to you," he added. "As a former New England choirboy, I was quite shocked at what I heard. One doesn't often hear such slurs as 'ninny' and 'stubborn baboon' uttered in polite society. Or, for that matter, in the sort of society I frequent."

Von Esh wasn't inside the place. There were only four booths and a counter. A girl with Jean Harlow hair was the only customer and she was sitting at the rearmost booth. When we came in, she looked up from the copy of *Photoplay* she was reading, then checked her wristwatch, frowned, and returned to the movie magazine. Behind the counter a plump, dark-haired young man in khaki trousers and a white sweatshirt was seated at a small butcher-block table and typing on an old portable with his forefingers.

Groucho and I settled at the counter.

He typed another line, then hopped up and came over to ask, "What'll you fellows have?"

"I suppose you're all out of cream puffs and lady fingers?" said Groucho.

"How about a jelly doughnut?"

"That's an intriguing question," observed Groucho. "If our panel of experts can't answer it in the allotted time, we'll be sending you a dozen mismatched volumes of the *Encyclopedia Britannica* and a really big box of chocolate-covered matzos."

"Groucho Marx," realized the counterman, straightening up and smiling.

"No, I'm sorry, that's not the correct answer. So now, while the orchestra plays a medley of tunes from the popular folk opera about life on a pig farm, *Porky and Bess*, you'll be sewn up in a snug burlap sack and dumped into the sea."

"It must be, you know, fate that brought you in here tonight, Mr. Marx." The young man pointed at his typewriter.

Groucho snapped his fingers. "Don't tell me. You've written a play."

"A motion picture script," he said. "I was just finishing up the final scene when you walked in."

"It has been the policy of the Marx clan, ever since we arrived on these sun-drenched shores from bonny Scotland, by way of a short detour through Bonnie Parker, never to look at anybody's movie scripts, my lad," Groucho informed him. "Might my amanuensis and I have some coffee?"

"I can see your point of view," the chubby counterman conceded. "Could I, you know, just tell you the basic notion— so as to get a professional opinion?"

Groucho narrowed his left eye, looked up at the low, grease-speckled ceiling. "Only if you can keep the whole wretched thing down to twenty-five words or less."

The young man grinned. "Let me think now," he said as he poured two mugs of coffee. "Okay, it goes like this. A pretty young girl inherits a bus line from an eccentric uncle she never met and she has to come to California from the Midwest to run it. She has all sorts of amusing adventures, falls in love with the guy who runs the rival bus line, outwits some crooks who want to use her buses for smuggling, and ends up rich and married. I call it *Love on a Bus*."

Groucho, very slowly, cleared his throat. "Ah, that's too bad. Another one of these inheriting-a-bus-line comedies, eh?" He gave a sad, sympathetic shake of his head. "I hate to tell you this, my boy, but there are already a half dozen very similar stories in production even as we speak. Isn't that true, Rollo?"

I nodded. "MGM is making a musical wherein Jeanette MacDonald inherits the Greyhound Bus Company and gets into a love-hate relationship with a handsome bus driver played by Nelson Eddy."

"Exactly. Rudolph Friml wrote the score for that one," said Groucho. "Over at Warners the Lane Sisters are gearing up to star in *Four Bus Drivers* and Edgar Bergen has just signed at Twentieth to star with Alice Faye in a screwball comedy about a ventriloquist's dummy who inherits a gondola. Not a bus in that case, but close. And, of course, Colonel Tim McCoy is already in production with one about a young miss who inherits a stagecoach line."

"Darn, it looks like I did it again," said the discouraged counterman. "Couple years back I had a swell idea about a rich playboy who pretended to be a butler and—"

"Ah," said Groucho as the door opened and Von Esh, bundled up in a long black overcoat and wearing a black beret, came stomping in out of the fog.

He tossed us a very brief nod before sitting in one of the booths.

Groucho said to the counterman, "Were I you, I'd change my story and have the young miss inherit a railroad."

"Hey, that's a terrific idea, Mr. Marx. Thanks."

"It is, yes." He gathered up his coffee mug and went over to join our informant.

I followed and we both sat facing Von Esh.

"This is very dangerous for me," he said.

"Wait'll you taste the coffee," said Groucho. "You'll really be frightened."

"I have to have fifty bucks to tell you where Henkel is hiding," he demanded in a low voice.

"Twenty was the price we agreed to," I reminded him.

"That was before all that violence at the rathskeller."

"Oh, that was merely a simple brawl, something you fun-loving Aryans enjoy," Groucho told him.

"Thirty," I said.

"Forty." He leaned forward, shoulders hunched.

"Thirty-five."

Von Esh made a resigned noise. "Very well. I don't want to hang around here arguing with you." He slid his hand, palm up, across the table.

Groucho nudged me. "Pay this lad out of petty cash, Rollo."

I had forty-one dollars in my wallet. "Where's Henkel?" I asked as I gave thirty-five of them to Von Esh.

Taking the money, he folded it and thrust it deep into a pocket of his overcoat. Then he pulled a paper napkin out of the dispenser and scrawled a few lines on it with his fountain pen.

Saying nothing more, he pushed the napkin across to me and eased free of the booth.

There was a Venice street address scrawled on the napkin.

Von Esh turned up his overcoat collar and hurried out of the Ebbtide.

Picking up the napkin, Groucho studied the address. "This isn't far from here," he said.

"More coffee?" called the counterman.

"No, thanks. We think one cup will be sufficient to kill all the cockroaches underfoot," said Groucho.

Beyond the streetcar tracks in Venice is the section of town that they tried, back some years ago, to make look like Venice,

189

Italy. Canals about ten or fifteen yards wide and three yards deep had been dredged in from the ocean. Arched bridges spanned the canals and houses and cottages were built facing the water. They never quite succeeded in capturing the essence of the original Venice and the canals were now full of stagnant water and whatever else floated in or was tossed in. Many of the houses had arrived at a ramshackle state and the land all around was marshy and overgrown.

The house where Henkel was supposed to be lying low sat on a weedy lot just a hundred feet or so in from the foggy Pacific. There were no lights showing, no cars parked anywhere near it.

Groucho left his Cadillac half a block away on the narrow street that ran along behind the dark cottage. "I do hope this isn't a trap," he said. "It'd be embarrassing to come to grief in such a shabby setting."

Opening the glove compartment, I took out a flashlight. "Tough to tell in this fog, but there doesn't seem to be anybody lurking around."

"One of the essential qualifications for lurking is to be unobtrusive."

"True," I agreed. "Suppose we sneak up on this place, being unobtrusive ourselves?"

"You think that'll work better than running straight at the joint with loud cries of 'Up the rebels!' do you?"

"Probably, yeah." I eased my door open and stepped out into the surrounding mist.

Groucho got out on his side. When I joined him, he complained, "Golly, I didn't realize it would be so difficult to tiptoe across this quicksand."

The weedy ground was pretty mushy. We worked our way

across it, staying close to the low fence on the far right of the forty-foot lot.

We crouched next to the two battered galvanized garbage cans that sat five feet from the back door and listened.

We heard foghorns calling and far down the street a couple of cats were involved in either fighting or romance. But from the house we didn't hear anything.

"Shall we venture inside and see if the elusive gaffer is slumbering therein?" suggested Groucho in a whisper.

Nodding, I padded up to the back door. The lock was a simple one and wouldn't be too difficult to pick. When I took hold of the knob to give it a cautious twist, it turned.

I pushed gingerly and, with a faint creak of hinges, the door swung open.

"That's a bad sign," whispered Groucho at my side. "Traditionally an unlocked portal means the intrepid investigators are going to find a bloody corpse or six sinister foreigners who're going to net them and sell them to a harem."

Ducked low, I crossed the dark threshold. I stood in the hallway for a few seconds, listening. I didn't hear anything, but the smells of stale beer and cooking fat were strong in the air.

After a few more silent seconds I risked clicking on the flash, keeping the beam pointed at the floor.

Groucho nudged me gently in the back. "Forward into the fray, Rollo," he urged quietly.

I followed the oval of light the flashlight made on the linoleum-covered floor into the front room of the cottage.

"Somebody on the floor," said Groucho, "over to the right there."

He swung the light. "Nope, it's only a bundle of clothes."

Neatly folded on the thin rug were a pair of dark trousers,

a blue work shirt, socks, an undershirt, and a pair of striped shorts. A pair of large work boots stood next to the clothes.

Pinned to the shirt was a note.

Genuflecting, I read it.

I am unable to live with my terrible guilt. I have decided to take my life. By the time you read this, I will have walked into the ocean to swim out until I become exhausted and drown. I killed Felix Denker, may God forgive me. Franz Henkel.

"Convenient." Groucho wandered over and sat on the sofa. The springs gave a mournful thunk.

"Yep, solves the Denker murder, eliminates the need to hunt for Henkel." I got out my handkerchief, used it to unpin and pick up the suicide note. "Same lettering style as all the other notes in our collection." I folded it away, carefully, in the pocket of my coat.

"Shouldn't we, Inspector Wade, leave the note? It is, after all, what one might call 'evidence.' "

"That would make it too easy for Erika Klein and her crew," I said. "Without the note all anybody else is going to find here is a bundle of laundry."

"Too bad those boots aren't my size, or we could swipe them, too." He stood up. "For the sake of thoroughness, Rollo, we'd best search the whole joint."

"Sure, even though we probably aren't going to find anything," I said. "I doubt whether Henkel ever actually hid out here."

We devoted nearly an hour to going over the cottage and didn't find anything else.

Twenty-five

Groucho yawned. "If I fall asleep at the wheel," he requested, "cover me with that quilt in the backseat." He rolled his window down a few inches and chill night fog came spilling in. "Ah, a few lungfuls of poisonous sea mist will buck me up, matey."

I yawned. "I've been thinking about that guy who was behind the counter at the Ebbtide," I said.

"Wholesome thoughts, I trust."

Foghorns were calling on our left.

"We tried to convince him to abandon his screenplay idea— and he probably will—but his basic notion was damned close to ours for *Cinderella on Wheels.*"

"Basic ideas are a dime a dozen," said Groucho. "No, wait. I was reading in the *Wall Street Journal* only last week that the price has shot up to two bits a dozen. But even so, Mr. Maugham, it's how we flesh out the idea that counts."

"But maybe the whole idea is trite and—"

"We're dwelling smack-dab in the middle of the triteness capital of the world," he reminded me.

I shrugged. "Could be I'm losing my confidence," I admitted. "Especially after our meeting with Lew Marker at Mammoth the other day."

"What you need, young feller, is a copy of my forthcoming book, *How to Win Friends and Influence Morons*," Groucho said, closing his window. "Lew Number Two is, and I say this at the risk of offending all the decent, God-fearing halfwits in Southern California, a halfwit."

"Yeah, but a halfwit who can okay our script."

Groucho asked, "Might I give you a little fatherly advice?"

"Shoot."

"All right, do your homework every night, mow the lawn once a week, and quit worrying because you're earning less than your wife right now."

"That does bother me some, yeah."

"I sensed that," he said. "Chiefly I sensed it because you babble about the fact from dawn to dusk and overtime on Saturdays."

"Okay, I'll continue to have faith in *Cinderella on Wheels*."

After a moment Groucho said, "And keep in mind that I already have a hit movie comedy script to my credit. I refer, of course, to that cinema classic of 1937, *The King and the Chorus Girl*."

"I keep getting those titles mixed up. Is that the one about the giant gorilla?"

"No, you're thinking of *King Lear*."

I said, "On *The King and the Chorus Girl* script you had Norman Krasna for a partner."

"Exactly, but even with a handicap like that, I turned out a socko movie."

"Krasna's got a hell of a lot more experience as a screenwriter than I do."

"Listen, Rollo, I happen to be an expert on latent talent—as well as blatant talent and latex talent—and, believe you me, you've got all three."

I asked, "Was that movie a hit?"

"More or less."

"I didn't much like the guy they got to star in it. Fernand Gravet, wasn't it?"

"A French import. I believe Warners got him along with a shipment of cheese they'd ordered for the commissary," he said. "I advised them to Americanize his name and call him Fred Gravy, but that was met with opposition. Joan Blondell was sure cute in that movie, though."

"She was," I agreed.

"And even when she wears lingerie, she manages to give the impression she isn't," he said. "That's what great acting is all about."

After a moment I said, "Do you think maybe we ought to do more work on our scenario and—"

"Not at all, my boy. In its present state, it is a gem of purest ray serene. I haven't the vaguest notion what that means, but I don't think we should mess with it."

I nodded, yawned again, and fell asleep in my seat.

Hooey," said Jane.

We were in the kitchen of our house and it was close to 2:00 A.M. After retrieving her, Groucho had dropped us at our home and driven off to Beverly Hills.

I was making a pot of cocoa. Jane was standing, arms folded, with her back to the icebox. "It's a basic instinct," I resumed, "from primordial times, that the male protects his mate from danger."

"And who protects you, ninny? You've already gotten yourself conked on the noggin," she reminded me, "and threatened with death and nearly stomped by a horde of Nazi goons."

"That's no reason why I should have let you come along to Venice, Jane. We didn't know what we might run into when—"

"Wait now, Clarence Darrow," my wife cut in, "you don't have a case. You and Groucho didn't get shot at in Venice or, from what you've told me, even encounter anybody at all. So I very well could have accompanied you instead of playing whist with Elena Sederholm and her insipid husband and some dull next-door neighbor named Sears Roebuck who—"

"Nobody's named Sears Roebuck."

"Well, somebody whose name sounds like that the way he mumbles," she said. "The point being that I was bored for a couple of hours while you guys were rendezvousing with German spies and wading in canals and having a—"

"Whist was probably a lot more exciting than anything we did," I told her. "What you have to keep in mind, Jane, is that I love you and I didn't want you to get hurt."

"Hooey," she said.

"This is where I came in." I took the cocoa off the burner.

Jane asked, "Is that an apology?"

"Sure, an abject one."

"Then I'll have a cup of cocoa," Jane said, smiling. "And I'll even sleep in the same bed with you."

"Gosh," I said.

Twenty-six

Groucho, hunched under a saggy black umbrella, was making his way from a parking lot at the Peaceable Woodlands Cemetery toward the Little Chapel of the Wayfarer. It was about fifteen minutes before 10:00 A.M. and heavy rain had been falling for over an hour now.

The church was small, modeled after something you might have found in an Irish village a century or more earlier. On a stretch of lawn across the street the police had set up half a dozen sawhorses, and five uniformed Glendale cops in rain gear were keeping back a crowd of about a hundred movie fans and tourists who'd come to Felix Denker's funeral in hopes of catching a glimpse of a star or two. Most of them were carrying umbrellas, although a few were using steepled copies of the *L.A. Times* to protect them from the hard morning rain.

Sergeant Norment, wearing a gray trench coat and a wide-brimmed black hat, was standing at the edge of the crowd, smoking a cigarette and watching the front of the church.

Nearing the Little Chapel, Groucho saw Irene Dunne and Randolph Scott climbing the imitation-marble steps. The crowd across the way made appreciative noises and a teenage boy with a newspaper umbrella tried to climb over a barrier to get a closer glimpse. He was stopped.

On Groucho's left now was a small grove of cypress trees. "Groucho, might I speak to you?" called a dapper man with a plaid umbrella.

It was Conrad Nagel, lurking among the trees.

Groucho climbed up across the soggy grass. "Conrad, what brings you out in weather like this?"

The fair-haired actor explained, "I've been invited to deliver a eulogy for my dear colleague Felix Denker."

"Your mellifluous oration will add to the solemnity of the occasion."

Touching Groucho's damp coat sleeve, Nagel continued, "I sincerely hope you won't think me overly sensitive, but . . ." He paused to clear his throat. "In the past, most notably that infamous occasion at Kahn's Egyptian Palace movie theater last year, you interrupted a presentation of mine."

"That was to solve a murder," reminded Groucho, "and bring the killer to justice."

The wind shifted suddenly, sending rain into their faces.

Nagel asked him, "But you don't intend to reveal the solution to poor Felix's murder here this morning, do you? You're not planning to pop up during my recitation and unmask a—"

"Conrad, you won't, I assure you, even know I'm inside the Little Chapel of the Wayfarer," promised Groucho. "Not until my banjo arrives."

His pale eyebrows rising, the actor took a step back. "Banjo?"

"Ah, apparently you haven't been informed as yet that it was Denker's last wish to have what is commonly known as a

New Orleans send-off?'' asked Groucho. "Therefore, a jazz band has been hired to play him to his final rest and I've been, which I find quite flattering, asked to sit in with the boys. Further, they've graciously suggested that I take a solo on the banjo, an instrument, I might add, that I only recently mastered thanks to a correspondence school course I took from an estimable institution based in Milwaukee, Wisconsin.''

"You're telling me a jazz band is intending to play at this—"

"Miff Mole and his group ought to be arriving at any moment.''

"Miff Mole? Who or what is—"

"Miff Mole heads up, not surprisingly, a group known as Miff Mole and His Bourbon Street Stompers.'' He consulted his wristwatch, then looked expectantly around. "They ought to being rolling in at any moment.''

"A brass band is going to spoil—"

"Tell you what, Conrad, I'll catch Miff before they go into the chapel and get him to promise they won't start stomping until you have completely and totally finished your piece. Fair enough?''

Nodding vaguely, Nagel headed away in the direction of the chapel.

Groucho noticed that only the hearse itself was parked in front of the little church. That meant the vehicle that had transported Erika Klein to the chapel was parked elsewhere, quite probably out in back of the place.

While he was making his way up the five slippery steps, somebody in the crowd asked, "Who's he?''

"Nobody,'' said several of the others.

Groucho stopped, turned, and walked back down to the

sidewalk. Cupping his hand to his mouth, he called, "That's all you guys know. I happen to be Mary Miles Minter, so there."

"Groucho Marx," cried the teenage boy, making another try to climb over a sawhorse.

Just before entering the church, Groucho folded up his umbrella and thrust it under his arm. Once inside, he stood at the back and scanned the crowded pews.

Erika Klein was sitting in the first row with the bald Gunther beside her. She was wearing a simple black dress and touching at her nose with a white lace handkerchief. Groucho headed for her.

Halfway down the aisle, someone hissed at him. He paused, noticing George Raft sitting there.

The actor motioned him over. When Groucho had bent close, Raft said, "I love that bus idea, pal."

"That's most gratifying. I'm delighted that you don't mind doing a whole movie in drag." He patted the actor on the shoulder and moved on.

He took hold of Erika's cold hand when he reached her side. "My deepest sympathies, my dear," he said in his most sincere voice, noticing that she didn't seem to have a purse with her. "I didn't realize until today how much I miss . . ." He stopped, shook his head sadly, and tugged out a pocket handkerchief. He blew his nose profoundly, made some sobbing sounds. "Forgive me for letting my emotions get the better of me, Erika."

Groucho skirted the altar and pushed out a side door of the chapel.

That put him, as he'd anticipated, close to the small parking lot at the rear of the chapel.

The limousine that had apparently brought Erika sat alone in the heavy rain. There was nobody anywhere near it.

Opening his umbrella again, Groucho slouched over to the sleek black vehicle and tried the back door.

The door opened silently and he peeked inside. "Yreka," he exclaimed, spotting a large black purse sitting on the backseat next to a folded copy of the *Los Angeles Times.*

When he slipped out of the car five minutes later, he had a memo in Erika's own hand and, for good measure, a short note written by Felix Denker, folded away in the breast pocket of his coat.

The door he'd exited from had apparently locked itself and so he had to go back around to the front of the chapel to enter again.

As he was ascending the steps this time, somebody across the street shouted, "It's Groucho again."

"No, that's Harpo this time," said somebody else. "I recognize the walk."

Groucho took a seat in the last pew at the rear. He noticed the flower-draped coffin sitting up on its wheeled cart on the altar now. "What a morbid thing to have at a funeral," he said to himself.

He scanned the crowd for a few minutes. Surprisingly he didn't spot Miles Ravenshaw anywhere. He'd expected the ham to be there, possibly dressed in his Sherlock Holmes costume and posing alongside the coffin.

But then he inhaled sharply. Sitting about ten rows ahead and across the aisle was Von Esh, the unreliable informer.

Dashiell Hammett opened the door and scowled out at us. "What the hell do you want?" he asked me. A lean, gray-haired man, he was standing in the doorway of the Tudor-style house in Westwood with a half-empty highball glass in his knobby left hand.

"This is Roger Connington's house, isn't it?" I said.

"Yeah. So what?"

"I came to see Clair Rickson."

"What makes you think she's got any great interest in seeing you?"

"When I talked to her on the phone an hour ago, she invited me to drop by at eleven."

Hammett was scrutinizing Jane now, looking her up and down. "Who's the dame?" he inquired.

"My wife and—"

"I also serve as his moll at times," put in Jane. "And I'm terrific at shorthand. Why don't you tell Miss Rickson that we're here, Mr. Hammett, and then fix yourself a cup of black coffee after you do that?"

He laughed a short barking laugh. "Jesus, a smart-ass broad," he said. "Thinks she can hold her own with men, tell them what to do. What a pain in the ass she must be."

Quietly I told him, "You're going to have a pain in the vicinity of the solar plexus if you don't get the hell out of the way and quit—"

"Dash, you mean-minded bastard, what are you up to now?"

"Mind your own damn business, Clair. I'm just chasing off a Fuller Brush man and his tootsie."

Behind Hammett appeared a fat, dark-haired woman in a bright Japanese kimono. She, too, was holding a cocktail glass but appeared somewhat more sober than her fellow writer. "Hey, good morning, Frank," she said in her froggy, cigarette-stained voice. "Don't mind Dash. He's always nasty when he's drunk. And since he's just about always drunk, he's about as much fun to have around as a bear with a sore tooth. He was a hell of a writer once, though."

"I still am, you sow." Hammett turned on his heel and retreated into the house. "And if you're going to attempt to insult me, honey, do it with fewer tired clichés, huh?"

"*The Glass Key* is the best mystery novel written so far in this century," Clair said, motioning us to come in. "Since he took up with that Hellman bitch he can't write a damn thing. I keep telling him to send her back to Arthur Kober, but Dash is too damn stubborn."

The living room had a beamed ceiling and a deep fireplace that looked big enough for roasting boars. Three large tapestries depicting religious pilgrimages in Chaucer's time decorated the stucco walls.

Hammett, his drink replenished, was sprawled in a wood and leather armchair with his feet up on a coffee table. Stretched out facedown, and apparently asleep, on a low leather sofa was Roger Connington. His right arm dangled over the side of the cushion, and just beyond the reach of his pudgy fingers lay an overturned glass with a splotch of spilled liquor spreading out from it.

"Poor Roger's got a touch of influenza," explained Clair, after sipping her drink. "Rum seems to help."

"He's looking fine," said Jane.

"You're Frank's wife, dear?"

"At the moment, but, this being Hollywood, I may move along any day now."

203

Clair smiled, a bit sadly. "I used to be bright and pretty once myself," she said. "But that—"

"Are you broads going to stand around cackling all day?" asked Hammett.

Clair took hold of my wife's arm. "C'mon, kids, we'll go into Roger's den and have our talk."

There was a suit of clothes stretched out on the shadowy hardwood hallway floor, looking as though whoever had been wearing it was suddenly sucked out of it magically. In dodging to avoid trodding on it, I nearly stepped on an empty Tanqueray gin bottle.

The den was a large lofty room with bookcases climbing up three of the walls. There were no books, though, and the only thing occupying any of the dusty shelves was a Betty Boop doll with a missing left ear. The room smelled of a great many dead cigars and also vaguely of fermenting grapes.

When Clair sat down on the leather sofa, the cushion made a loud plopping sound. "What a life," she sighed.

I settled into an armchair and Jane sat on its arm, resting her hand on my shoulder. "As I mentioned on the telephone, Clair, Groucho and I—"

"How is Groucho?"

"Tip-top. He's attending Felix Denker's funeral and—"

"What a farce that is," said the heavyset writer. "Erika never gave a shit about him and they weren't even living together anymore. People get so taken up with the goddamned proprieties that they—"

"You've talked to the police, to Sergeant Norment?"

"Sure, but I couldn't tell him one hell of a lot, Frank." She took a long swig of her drink. "But at least I don't think I'm a suspect. Do you and Groucho have any idea who killed Felix?"

"We're working on it," I said. "Why were you there on the set, Clair?"

When she shrugged, the ice cubes rattled in her glass. "Damned if I know," she answered. "I'd had a quarrel with Roger and, well, I got angry and then tipsy. Next thing I knew I was sitting in that London pub with my bottle of scotch."

"What time'd you get there?"

"That's exactly what your cop pal wanted to know," Clair said. "Must have been two, three in the morning."

"Meaning Denker was long since dead."

"I didn't see his body, I didn't hear anything, didn't see a damn thing," she said. "I wandered onto that set, maybe because it reminded me of a saloon. Sat around feeling very sorry for myself until I drank myself into a stupor. Came the dawn, a police doctor was sticking smelling salts up my nose."

"You wrote the Sherlock Holmes script," said Jane. "Were you around the set much?"

"A few times," she replied. "I was supposed to be writing some piece of tripe called *Curse of the Zombies*, so I had to pretend to be in my office most days."

"Friend of ours is going to be the voodoo priest in that," I mentioned.

"Enery McBride," she said, smiling. "A nice guy and a swell actor."

Jane asked, "Did Erika Klein visit her husband much during the filming?"

"Only once or twice while I was around." She frowned at me. "Do you and Groucho think dear Erika did her hubby in?"

"She's on our suspect list," I admitted. "What sort of conversations did they—"

"I never heard her say, 'I'm going to shoot you dead some

night, dearest,' " Clair assured me. "Usually she'd complain that he hadn't sent her a check for her expenses or tell him his jacket needing pressing. Mild nagging, they call that."

"Did you talk much with Denker?"

"Quite a bit, sure," she answered. "But after he shelved our project, I didn't see him much."

"What project—another movie?"

"No, Felix had the notion he wanted to do a book of memoirs," Clair explained. "Dealing with his life and career back in Germany. *A Movie Director in Nazi Germany* was our working title. With all the interest in Hitler and the impending World War, it would've sold, I'm sure."

"He wanted you," asked my wife, "to help him write it?"

"Yeah, because poor Felix didn't feel exactly comfortable in English. He was going to dictate stuff to me, a lot of it based on his journals."

I sat up. "Denker kept journals?"

"So he told me. Made an entry every blessed day from about 1925 to 1933."

"Did you see them?"

She shook her head. "Nobody saw them, Frank," she said. "I only heard about them. Whenever I asked Felix if I could take a gander at these fabled books, he told me he wasn't ready to let anyone see them. There was a lot of personal stuff in there that he didn't want to put into his public memoirs. Even when I told him that I don't read German all that well, he refused."

"Where are those books?"

"God only knows."

"Didn't he keep them at his house?"

Clair said, "No, because I don't think he wanted Erika to

206

get her hands on them. He had them stored someplace, but I never found out where."

"But Erika knew about them?"

"She must have if the guy was making entries in them every day."

I glanced up at Jane. "There'd be details of any sort of deals he made in Germany in those journals," I said.

"They'd make interesting reading, yes."

"Why," I asked Clair, "did he abandon the idea of writing his memoirs?"

"I'm not sure," she said. "He just told me one day that he'd decided it wasn't a good idea to continue. My impression is something scared him off, but I have no idea what. Too bad, because it would've made an interesting—"

The telephone on Connington's desk started ringing.

With a grunt, Clair rose off the sofa and caught up the receiver. "Top of the morning," she said, and listened for a couple of minutes. "Yeah, that's typical of him, Ray. I'll pass along the message. Bye now."

She hung up, walked to the doorway.

Into the hall she shouted, "Dash, you irresponsible bastard. Ray Chandler says you were supposed to meet him and Erle Gardner at the Copper Skillet on Gower for breakfast a full goddamn hour ago."

"Screw them," called Hammett.

Twenty-seven

The coffin came rolling down the aisle of the Little Chapel of the Wayfarer and out into the rain. After being loaded into the hearse, it would be driven a quarter of a mile downhill to the Denker gravesite.

The mourners began to rise and make their way out of the quaint little church.

Groucho remained standing beside his pew, eyes on Von Esh. The crew-cut informant didn't join the procession either. After letting the others on his bench step out over him, he went sliding on his backside to the opposite end of the pew.

Then he hopped up, hurrying toward a side door and out of the church.

Groucho, crouched slightly, dodged the stream of people leaving the place.

As he headed for the rear of the church George Raft prodded him in the ribs. "Don't forget that swell script, pal," he urged.

"It's etched in memory, Georgie."

By the time Groucho had worked his way around to the opposite aisle and then out of the chapel, Von Esh was trotting toward the crest of a hill.

It was Groucho's intention to catch up with him and persuade him to tell him who'd suggested that he send us to find that fake suicide note last night.

When Groucho reached the top of the incline, he didn't see any sign of his quarry. Stretching out below him was one of the more expensive sections of the cemetery. There were ornate tombstones stretched out for over a half acre, and winged angels abounded, as did marble tombs. Dotting the clipped grass were stands of weeping willows.

The wind caught his umbrella and Groucho was pulled to his left.

He stumbled, looked around again.

He spotted Von Esh now, far below and jogging along beside a row of gravestones.

Increasing his pace, Groucho took off in pursuit.

He was opposite an especially imposing Angel Gabriel when he heard an odd rushing noise. That was followed by a clinking, and then a chunk of Gabriel's widespread wing leaped off and whacked against the side of Groucho's head.

He flung his umbrella away and threw himself flat out on the wet grass.

A second rifle shot knocked the nose clean off a cherub who decorated a gravestone not more than three feet from where Groucho had splashed down.

As we were driving along Bayside Boulevard, heading homeward, the rain started to hit down harder. "Want to stop somewhere for lunch?" I asked Jane.

"It's a shame about Hammett," she said.

"You still brooding about that?"

"I read *The Maltese Falcon* when I was in high school and I loved it."

"You should've told him that. Maybe it would've persuaded him to take the pledge."

"Well, it's a marvelous book."

"From time to time a drunk writes a marvelous book. It has something to do with some rule Darwin discovered some years ago."

"You're still angry because he was rude to me."

"He was rude to everybody within a mile of him."

She was quiet for a moment.

The rain drummed on the roof of the car, our tires made sizzling noises on the wet street.

Very quietly she began to cry.

I asked, "You upset with me for some reason?"

She shook her head, sniffling. "No, you're okay."

"Good, thanks for the testimonial. So why are you crying?"

"He reminded me of my father."

I glanced over at her. "You've never really told me much about your father."

"I haven't, no."

"I know he drank some, too."

"He drank one hell of a lot. He was an alcoholic."

"I didn't know that," I mentioned. "Which, when you consider the fact that we're married, is sort of odd."

She took a lace-trimmed handkerchief out of her purse. She wiped at her eyes, blew her nose, wadded the handkerchief up in a tight ball. "Sometime, Frank, I'll tell you all about my father."

"Fine."

"But not today."

Up ahead the traffic signal flashed to red.

I hit the brakes and stopped at the corner right next to the big outdoor newsstand.

Under the slanting green-and-white awning a middle-aged newsboy was hollering something.

Jane rolled down her window.

"Extra! Extra!" the chunky man shouted. "Sherlock Holmes disappears!"

"We better buy a paper," suggested Jane.

Using his elbows, Groucho, still stretched out flat on his stomach, was working his way toward a crypt some ten feet away. He hoped that would offer him some shelter from the rifleman who was intent on plugging him.

"Although I suppose this is as good a place as any to cash in one's chips," he reflected. "They'd only have to drag my lifeless corpse a few dozen yards to toss it into a grave. That would cut way down on expenses and—"

Another rifle shot came whizzing by overhead. Overhead in this case was about three feet above the ground. The slug hit a tombstone immediately to Groucho's right and gouged out part of the *M* in the chiseled word *Memory.*

"Usually in shooting galleries it's only three shots for a dime."

He felt very cold and soggy as he inched along.

A brass urn jumped off the tombstone he was crawling past. The urn leaped free, went spinning into the air, and smacked against the wing of a marble angel.

"That's five shots now. But, fortunately, no prize yet."

Up to his right someplace, from a totally different direction, two shots sounded.

Groucho increased the speed of his crawl and dragged himself behind the sheltering wall of the ornately carved crypt.

He heard running footsteps now and three more gunshots. But nobody seemed to be firing at him any longer.

"Is that you cringing behind there, Marx?"

Groucho waited a few seconds and then peeked out. "Sergeant Norment of the Burbank Constabulary, what a jolly surprise," said Groucho, rising and stepping out into the open. "Did you shoot the chap who was shooting at me?"

"Nope, he got clean away," said Jack Norment. "When we heard the shooting I deserted the burial ceremonies and came back here to see what was going on." He eyed Groucho. "Apparently you've annoyed somebody again."

"It has to be that, Sergeant, since Marx-hunting season doesn't open officially for nearly three months yet."

Sitting atop a tombstone, Norment asked, "Any idea why somebody would want to kill you?"

"Besides *Room Service*, you mean?" Groucho spread his hands wide and shrugged. "No, I lead such a blameless life that, last time I heard, the pope was planning to have me canonized as Saint Julius."

"Those Nazis and Boy Storm Troopers you got into a brawl with last night at Siegfried's wouldn't have a grudge against you, huh?"

"Oh, that was nothing more than adolescent prankishness."

"And I don't suppose you're close enough to knowing who murdered Denker to be dangerous to anybody?"

"I'm a mere amateur, as you pointed out yourself, Sergeant."

"Amateurs get killed, too, Marx," he warned. "You've already missed your chance to toss a handful of dirt on Denker's coffin. So what say I escort you to your car and you go away?"

"That's a jolly suggestion," said Groucho, linking his arm with the policeman's. "I don't know about you, but whenever I'm traipsing around over several hundred buried bodies, I just get the wimwams something awful. Especially after somebody with a rifle tries to bag me."

Twenty-eight

I told the secretary who answered M. J. McLeod's phone, "This is Richard Harding Davis of the *Denver Post.* I'd like to speak with Miss McLeod."

"She's out of the office right now, Mr. Davis."

"Any idea when she'll be back?"

"I'm afraid not. Would you like to have her telephone you at the newspaper?"

"I'm out of the office, too. I'll have to try her again. Thanks."

From her studio Jane called, "Isn't your old sweetie there?"

"Nope. Guess I'll have to try her at the heart-shaped love nest I've installed her in." I dialed Mary Jane's home number.

On the fifth ring a voice that wasn't hers answered. "Miss McLeod's service."

"I'd like to get in touch with her."

"She should be checking in eventually, if you'd care to leave a message."

"Tell her Richard Harding Davis wants to talk to her. She has my number."

I hung up, left the sofa, and wandered in to where my wife

was working at her drawing board. "No luck yet," I reported.

"When you do contact her, Frank, she's just going to confirm what we already think happened."

"Probably, sure, but I'd like to get Mary Jane to tell me directly: 'Yep, it's only a publicity dodge, because Ravenshaw doesn't have the vaguest idea of who done it.' "

"That has to be what's going on," said Jane. "He hasn't got anything to announce at his party, so he's pretending he was abducted by the forces of evil."

"That sounds like the sort of thing Mammoth's publicity head, Randy Grothkopf, and Ravenshaw would come up with to get off the hook, yeah," I agreed. "Sherlock will lie low for a few days, then reappear and claim he just managed to escape from his kidnappers. Considering how dangerous investigating the Denker case has turned out to be, he owes it to his family and his public to retire from the case."

"You and Groucho believe that Erika Klein is the killer," said Jane, setting down her pen and pushing back from the board. "But she's only taken care of people who could do her serious harm. Nobody can possibly consider Miles Ravenshaw a formidable threat."

I went around on her side of the drawing board. "Judging by the newspaper story, the whole thing sounds like a plan of Ravenshaw and Grothkopf," I said. "Ravenshaw left home this morning, telling his wife he was going to attend Felix Denker's funeral. Seemingly he never got to Glendale and nobody's seen him since."

"Because he drove somewhere else to hide," said Jane, pointing at the drawing she'd been working on. "What do you think of this?"

"Hollywood Molly in her underwear?"

216

"I've been thinking of adding paper dolls to the Sunday page," Jane explained. "Say once a month or so. How's that sound?"

"We're seeking an honest opinion here?"

"As opposed to what?"

"Mindless husband approval."

"C'mon, nitwit. I want your *opinion*, not a publicity release."

"Paper dolls are okay for *Jane Arden* or *Toots* and *Casper*," I said. "But *Hollywood Molly* is too smart a strip for that kind of stuff."

"I always liked paper dolls when I was a kid," she said. "My Fresno aunt used to bring me books of them and I'd cut out the dolls and dress them up for hours. I especially like dressing them in bridal clothes."

"Let's save that for our next session, Mrs. Denby," I said.

"You're telling me that cute paper dolls are going to cheapen my strip?"

"Well, basically, yeah, in my opinion, Jane."

"Well, in my opinion, you don't know your backside from your elbow."

"I bet I do. When they asked me that question on my state driver's license test last year, I answered it correctly," I assured her. "My backside is the one with the flashing red light."

"If I added paper dolls, it would broaden my audience. Thousands of little girls would flock to *Molly*."

"It's already the most popular strip your syndicate's had in five years, Jane."

"Paper dolls are very popular right now."

"So are crossword puzzles, but you don't have those in your comic strip either."

"I may stick one in just to spite you." Jane paused to take a deep breath in and out. "Let's get back to the vanishing Sherlock Holmes. You sounded like you might actually believe he was abducted."

"I don't, no," I told her. "But I don't want to make the mistake of not looking into the possibility that maybe there was foul play. That's what detectives, and reporters, do. Check all the possibilities."

"Well, your former true love can settle that question once you get in touch with her."

"Listen, just because I used to frolic naked in mountain meadows with Mary Jane McLeod, you can't go labeling her my—"

The telephone rang.

Jane picked up the extension on her taboret. "Hello?" She listened for a moment. "No, he's fully clothed at the moment, Groucho. Although he did just return from frolicking jaybird naked in a nearby mountain meadow." She listened again. "Yes, we've heard about Ravenshaw's alleged disappearance. No, we didn't know somebody tried to shoot you." Frowning, Jane handed me the receiver.

"Who tried to shoot you, Groucho?" I asked.

"We're offering a prize of one hundred dollars in cash and two hundred dollars in frilly underwear to the first person to come up with an answer. As usual, neatness, originality, and aptness of theme count. Though not for a hell of a lot." He then told me about what had befallen him at the Peaceable Woodlands Cemetery while he was attending the Denker funeral. "I did manage, before the target practice commenced, to glom on to some nifty handwriting samples. I'd like to have you and your keen-eyed missus drop over for a powwow. Or you can have a large slice of cheesecake instead of the pow-wow. It's up to youse."

"What time?"

"I'm currently languishing alone here at the Château d'If, because my family has scattered to the four winds," he replied. "And since there are only three of them, one of the winds is going to get short shrift. But, as Benjamin Franklin so wisely put it, better a short shrift than something I intend to think of later in your shorts."

"An hour?"

"I'll instruct one of the serfs to let down the drawbridge, Rollo," he promised. "I could add that it'll probably be Bennett Cerf, but lately I've come to realize that these literary allusions seem to go right over your head. And another thing that's been going over your head is that wool cap I knitted for you back during the—"

"Good-bye, Groucho," I mentioned and hung up.

Twenty-nine

The rain had diminished to a fuzzy drizzle by the time we arrived at Groucho's home on North Hillcrest Drive in Beverly Hills.

Before Jane and I reached the front door, it was yanked open. "I'm afraid you're too late to tune the harpsichord," said Groucho. "It passed away just minutes ago."

"Well, at least we can see it gets a decent burial," I said as Jane and I went into the hosue.

Groucho was wearing one of his ancient bathrobes and a pair of shaggy bunny rabbit slippers. "Good evening, Lady Jane, you're looking extremely presentable," he said. "I must warn you, however, that your reputation will suffer if you continue to be seen in public with rustic yokels such as the one you have in tow this evening."

"I know, yes," said Jane, who was carrying a file folder in her left hand. "Just before we left home we got a phone call from the Rockefeller attorneys informing me I've been disinherited."

"Think how much worse it would've been were you related

to the Rockefeller family in some way." Making a follow-me gesture, he headed for the kitchen.

Once inside his big yellow-and-white kitchen, we sat around the table.

Groucho had a legal tablet, two stubby pencils, and a pewter mug at his place. "This contains eggnog," he explained, tapping the metal cup. "In my native Petrograd we believe anything with a stiff shot of brandy in it will ward off chills, fever, and ague. We believe this, mind you, even though we haven't the vaguest notion what ague is and aren't even sure how to pronounce it."

"Frank said you were crawling around a damp cemetery," said Jane, "while they were shooting at you."

"Like Napoléon's army, I was traveling on my stomach." He drank some of his spiked eggnog.

"It wasn't Von Esh who was doing the shooting, huh?" I said.

"Our old drinking companion was functioning much like the mechanical rabbit that gets greyhounds to trot around the track," he said. "Someone else was doing the shooting."

"But you didn't see who?"

"Unless it was a marble angel, no."

Jane stood up. "Forgive me for behaving like your typical Beverly Hills matron, Groucho, but would you mind if I fixed a pot of coffee?"

"Ah, excuse me, child, I should've brewed a pot while awaiting your arrival," he apologized. "But I got so wrapped up in playing a one-handed game of honeymoon bridge that I quite forgot. Next week, by the way, I'm going to get wrapped in the prettiest Christmas paper you've ever seen. My stationer's a bit deaf and originally he thought I'd ordered Chris-

222

tian paper and he sent over six back issues of the *Christian Science Monitor.*"

"I'll make coffee." Jane went into the pantry and emerged with a can of Orem Bros. coffee, left over from the supply the original sponsor of our defunct radio show had given Groucho the year before.

"I haven't been able to get through to Mary Jane McLeod," I said. "But I'm pretty sure she'll confirm that Ravenshaw's disappearance is a fake."

"Precisely, Rollo. The poor hambone hasn't come up with a solution, so he's going to remain incommunicado until wiser heads solve the mystery." He tapped a few bars of something that sounded like "Jeepers Creepers" on the side of his mug with the eraser end of one of his pencils. "I hope to have some important information on that very topic before the evening is very much older."

"Such as?" I asked him.

"If you intend to fill the vacancy we have for a Trappist monk, Rollo, you are going to have to learn patience," he advised. "Might be a good idea to learn several other card games as well, because there's just no telling how long we're likely to be marooned."

"You know something," accused Jane while measuring out ground coffee into the pot.

"All in good time, Penelope."

"I thought you had a smug expression on your face when we got here tonight," she said.

"Please, I beg of you, don't allude to one of the great tragedies of my life," he said. "You see, as a youth I was kidnapped by Gypsies and, using mostly rusty surgical instruments, they carved upon my face a permanent smug expression. You may

223

have read of my tragic fate in Victor Hugo's epic novel *The Man Who Smirked.* Two seasons ago the tale appeared briefly on Broadway as the musical *Hugo Your Way, I'll Go Mine.* Kenny Baker starred, along with Phil Baker, Wee Bonnie Baker, and the Light Crust Dough Boys."

Setting the coffee pot on a burner, Jane asked, "Changing the subject, do you have that sample of Erika Klein's writing handy?"

"Right here, Scarlet, honey." He pulled two small sheets of paper from between the pages of his legal pad.

He held one up and Jane came to look at it over his shoulder. "I think so, yes." Taking the purloined memo written by Erika, she sat down and opened her folder.

"I also," said Groucho, flickering the other slip of paper, "picked up a sample of Denker's penmanship. It might come in handy, though I can't for the life of me think how at the moment."

"Speaking of Denker's writing," I said, "Clair Rickson told us he kept a journal for years. He'd been thinking about having her help him write a book about his years as a movie director in Germany."

Groucho's eyebrows climbed higher. "A thorough, day-by-day journal this would be?"

"So he told Clair, although she never saw an actual volume," I answered. "For some reason—and maybe he decided a memoir of those years might annoy Erika and her Nazi bosses—he gave up the idea."

"And where, pray tell, are those journals now?"

"Nobody knows. Or at least Clair doesn't," I said. "She doesn't think Erika does either."

"It's quite possible that Denker made notes in the pages of

his journals on all the juicy details of the deal he made to let them pass Dr. Helga Krieger off as Erika Klein."

I nodded agreement. "If we can find them, then we'll have some concrete proof of part of our theory."

Groucho, tongue poked into his cheek, was leaning back studying his kitchen ceiling. He then looked across at Jane. "What's the verdict, Rapunzel?"

"I don't think you could prove it to a court's satisfaction," she answered, "but I'm pretty near certain that if Erika Klein wrote this note you swiped, then she also lettered every darn one of the threatening notes in our file."

Groucho handed me the Denker sample. "Pass this to your spouse, Rollo."

I did.

Taking the note, Jane scanned it briefly. "So?"

"How difficult would it be to imitate that handwriting of Denker's?"

"Not very. It looks like he studied calligraphy at some point."

"Could you do it?"

"Heck yes, it wouldn't be that much of a challenge. But why?"

Groucho said, "Oh, it simply occurred to me that if we couldn't find any of the volumes of the actual journal, why, we might want to produce a few pages on our own."

I smiled. "Keep in mind it's all written in German."

"As I understand forgery, young fellow, it can be done in most any language."

"I studied German in school," said Jane.

"There you are," said Groucho, rubbing his palms together. "For first-class chicanery there's nothing like a forger with a college diploma. Of course, there's always the possibility that the diploma itself is—oops."

Someone had started using the knocker on his front door.

Groucho left his chair. "My, the pilgrims are flocking to the shrine tonight." He slouched out into the hall.

Jane said, "This could be the cause of the smug expression arriving."

We heard the door being opened and then Groucho exclaimed, "Why, Dr. Watson, as I live and breathe, what a ripping surprise."

Randell McGowan said, "Deuced informal this, what? Meeting round the kitchen table is beastly casual, but quite American, don't you know?"

"He can't help talking like this," explained Groucho in an apologetic tone.

Chuckling, the actor picked up the cup of coffee that Jane had just served him. "Thought you did a smashing job writing Groucho's radio show, Denby, old man. It was, yes, decidedly top-hole."

"Thanks. We enjoyed you in *The Secret Love of Queen Victoria.*"

"Very impressive whiskers," added Jane, returning to her chair. "If they gave an Academy Award for facial hair, you'd be a shoo-in."

"Oh, I say, what a droll young woman," said McGowan, chuckling again.

"Before we all succumb to Anglophobia," suggested Groucho, "you better fill us in on what you alluded to during our recent telephone conversation, Randell, old chap."

"As Groucho may have mentioned to you, Miles Raven-shaw is not a particular favorite of mine," said the actor after sampling his coffee. "I felt from the start that this business about his pretending to solve the murder of Felix Denker was a bit thick, you know." He drank more coffee. "I happen to be on friendly terms with Ravenshaw's valet. Chap named Denis Truett, whom I fagged for at Oxford. Denis fell on bad times some years back and went into service. Bloody shame, but there it is."

Groucho asked, "This Truett knows where Ravenshaw is hiding out?"

"Oh, yes, because Denis is with him, you see."

"Amplify that statement," Groucho requested.

The portly actor leaned back, hooking his thumbs in his waistcoat pockets and thereby increasing his resemblance to Dr. Watson. "Roughly two hours ago Denis telephoned me—without his master's knowledge, I hasten to add—to let me know he wouldn't be able to keep his luncheon appointment with me for tomorrow," he said. "He'd been enlisted to drive Ravenshaw to a cabin he'd rented up near Santa Barbara and then look after him while they hide out there."

"Then Ravenshaw is definitely in hiding so he won't have to announce his solution to the murder tomorrow night at his Christmas party?" I said.

The actor laughed. "The old boy's in an absolute fog, a mental pea-souper, don't you know, so far as the murder goes, my lad," he said. "Yes, he came up with this spurious kidnapping plot to extricate himself from a sticky situation. According to Denis, Ravenshaw will emerge from hiding sometime next week with a cock-and-bull story he's hoping the newspapers and the police will accept."

"How's his wife feel about his screwing up her party?" inquired Jane.

McGowan said, "The lady is in an absolute funk, my dear. She dotes on these extravagant soirees of theirs, you know. You can imagine how scared Ravenshaw is of facing the music when he'll risk her ire."

Groucho asked him, "Where exactly is this woodsy hide-away?"

"In a rustic area up above Santa Barbara," answered the actor, rubbing a knuckle across his military mustache. "I can provide you the address, should you need it."

"Provide away, old bean," invited Groucho. "I'm thinking we may want to make certain Ravenshaw is actually stowed away there."

"Oh, so?" I said.

"And," added Groucho, "we might want to make absolutely sure he remains there until after I have my press conference on Sunday."

"Press conference, old chap?" McGowan looked at him with interest. "Is one to assume, then, that you have succeed where Ravenshaw's failed?"

"Yes indeed, we've got the solution to everything," Groucho assured him.

"And you have proof?"

Groucho nodded in Jane's direction. "By Sunday we'll have a stack of it."

Thirty

Early Saturday morning Groucho and I were heading up the Coast Highway in my Ford. The day was clear and warm; on our left the Pacific Ocean was growing continually brighter.

We drove by a fruit juice stand shaped like a giant orange and then one shaped like a giant lemon.

"When you sight one shaped like a giant cabbage, Rollo, pull over," Groucho told me. "I want to fill my thermos bottle with borscht."

"It'll have to be purple," I said, "otherwise all you can get will be sauerkraut."

"Speaking of sour krauts, I . . . no, never mind." He unwrapped a fresh cigar. "I was going to make a rude remark about Erika Klein. But then I decided it was beneath me. You can well imagine how low something that's beneath me must be."

Out of the water a glaringly white yacht was sailing by, headed south. A gaggle of seagulls was flying in its wake, diving and swirling.

"Let that be a lesson to you," observed Groucho. "If you want to draw a crowd, scatter a little garbage around."

"You still planning to have your press conference tomorrow?"

"At precisely high noon, when all the decent citizens of Hollywood are getting up for breakfast."

"Where?"

"Two-twenty-one-B Baker Street strikes me as an appropriate location." He lit his cigar, rolling down the window on his side to blow a swirl of smoke out into the brightening morning.

I grinned. "How are we going to get back on the Mammoth lot?"

"That's being arranged." He puffed on his cigar, leaning back in the seat.

"Okay, so tell me how."

"As rosy-fingered dawn was tiptoeing in on little fairy brogans, I put in a call to none other than my brother Chico, also known as the fun-loving Rover Boy," he explained. "Chico, I realized, often plays bridge with Lew Goldstein, and Lew Number One happens to owe my ne'er-do-well sibling a favor. Chico will get the embargo lifted."

"Okay, but then—"

"Zeppo will team up with Nan to see that everyone on the guest list we concocted last night at the Marx hacienda accepts an invitation to attend. Oh, and I also called Sergeant Norment to inform him he'd be wise to see to it that we get a full house."

"And Norment's going to cooperate?"

"He apparently hasn't run the killer of Felix Denker to ground and, since I implied we'd likely be doing that come Sunday, he went along with my scheme," said Groucho. "He did, however, speak to me harshly at times and used words that I haven't heard since I left the convent."

I said, "Meanwhile Jane should be able to do her part of what's needed."

"Of that I have no doubt."

We'd dropped Jane off at Elena Sederholm's again, since I didn't feel it was safe for her to be home by herself. She was reluctant to do that, but together Groucho and I succeeded in persuading her that she had to work on her project. I also pointed out that most people don't play whist until after sundown and that we intended to gather her up long before that.

"The last couple of times a case called for exploring the wilderness," I said, "Jane and I did that together. So there's another reason she's somewhat annoyed."

"Any woman who knowingly marries you, Rollo, has to be prepared to spend at least part of her life in a state of annoyance."

"And we got to use Dorgan to help us in our tracking," I added. "Jane really likes that dog."

"Ah, yes, Dorgan, the renowned bloodhound and motion picture performer," said Groucho, puffing on his cigar. "One of the nicest fellows in the movies."

"Not that I don't enjoy working with you, Groucho," I assured him. "But with Dorgan there's that—"

"No need to continue; I fully understand the bond between a boy and his dog," he said. "I myself have seen every Rin Tin Tin movie and serial ever made. In fact, I attended so many dog movies that they had to have me sprayed for fleas."

The morning grew warmer and by the time we reached the outskirts of Santa Barbara, we were enjoying the kind of December day that people move west from Illinois for.

"You know where to turn off?" inquired Groucho.

"We want the next road on the right, yeah."

After I made the turn and we were driving up through unsettled wooded acres, Groucho said, "The other night at Siegfried's Rathskeller."

"An unsettling experience."

He nodded slowly. "There are quite a few people like Jack O'Banyon in Hollywood, although they don't, most of them, wear uniforms advertising it," he said. "That's why the Hillcrest is the only country club I can belong to."

"It's not going to change, not for a long time," I said. "There are just too many assholes in the world."

"So far the Silver Shirts haven't taken over out here," he said. "Otherwise I'd have to go around with a star pinned to my coat and tip my hat to the likes of O'Banyon." He grimaced. "There are terrible things happening in the world and . . ." His voice trailed off. "I don't know, Frank, you can join the Anti-Nazi League and support all the liberal causes and go to rallies and make a speech now and then, but a whole lot of Jews are going to get killed anyway."

Groucho snuffed his cigar in the ashtray, threw it out into the sunshine.

After a moment he tugged out his pocket handkerchief and blew his nose.

"Shit," he said quietly.

Thirty-one

We parked the car about a quarter mile beyond the dirt road that led down to the cabin where Ravenshaw was avoiding the public, leaving it off the roadway near a stand of pepper trees.

Trudging back through the warm morning, Groucho and I cut into the woods while we were still several hundred yards from the trail to the cabin.

Once in among the trees, we attempted to move as quietly as possible.

A loud thrashing sounded off on our right as we descended.

"Do mountain lions," inquired Groucho, "inhabit this part of the country?"

"Don't they pretty much restrict themselves to mountains?"

"The newspapers are continually running accounts about how a mountain lion wandered into a garden party in Bel Air or Beverly Hills and gobbled up the hostess and several dress extras."

"Well, I doubt a mountain lion would find either one of us palatable."

"Myself, I'm a mite fuzzy on the culinary habits of mountain lions," admitted Groucho as he slouched downhill through the brush. "I was only a wee lad when last I perused *Wild Animals I Have Known.* Although recently I've been contemplating turning out a book of memoirs to be entitled *Wild Animals I Have Married.*"

We continued in silence for a while.

I put out a restraining hand, saying quietly, "That's the cabin down through the trees there."

"Smoke coming out of the chimney," observed Groucho. "Plus a yellow Duesenberg convertible coupe in the garage. It's unlikely that a group of forest-dwelling rustics would drive a Duesenberg."

"No, we're obviously dealing with upper-class rustics here, Groucho." I nodded toward our right. "If we cut over that way and then go skulking through the woods, we ought to be able to come up pretty close to the side of the cabin without being spotted."

"Lead on, Dan Beard."

We heard the thrashing again, but it sounded farther away.

The cabin was large, built of logs, with a slanting tar paper roof. It didn't look exactly like an authentic woodland cabin but more like something a crew from a movie studio had put up. There was a screened porch running along the front of it and a sizable wooden bin for holding garbage cans on the side we were surreptitiously approaching.

While we were still about ten feet from the cabin, we started hearing a voice talking loudly. Hunching low, we worked our way closer.

". . . bloody hell did you allow that to happen, Randy?"

"Bingo, that's the ham himself," whispered Groucho.

"Yeah, talking to Randy Grothkopf, Mammoth's publicity chief."

Like all hideaways that catered to Hollywood, this one came equipped with a telephone.

". . . going to make me look like an absolute ass," the Sherlock Holmes actor was complaining. "How the devil could Lew Number One have given Groucho permission to set foot on the studio grounds tomorrow and use *my* sets to stage some shabby . . . Well, then, I'm not especially pleased, old man, that they think more of Groucho's vulgar imitation-Italian brother than they do of me. *The Valley of Fear* is, after all, a big-budget production that . . . Well, a middle-budget production. Keep in mind, dear boy, that it was *your* bloody idea that I make all those outrageous claims about solving . . . Yes, yes, I know what the original plan was, Randy. I stay out of sight until the police do the actually work of clearing up the murder. Then I pop up, give them the ridiculous story that I was kidnapped but actually knew the solution even before they did. Why in the name of . . ."

Close to my ear, Groucho said, "Well, Sir Rollo, that confirms our worst suspicions."

"It does, yeah," I agreed. "So let's wend our way back to the car and—"

"That Duesenberg sitting in the garage."

"What about it?"

"Could you incapacitate the vehicle in some quick and simple way?"

"That wouldn't be a problem, but—"

"In case Ravenshaw, who now knows about my press conference of the morrow, decides to return to civilization and try to screw things up for us," Groucho explained, "it would be jolly comforting to know that he was stranded here with a car that might take a couple days to fix."

"All right," I agreed. "We'll work our way around the back of his cabin, sneak silently into the garage, and while Ravenshaw is still squabbling on the telephone, I'll remove the distributor cap."

"Let us begin," urged Groucho.

We were able to do everything I'd outlined in less than ten minutes.

As I was wiping my greasy hands on my pocket handkerchief, however, a lean middle-aged man holding a .45 automatic appeared in the open garage doorway.

"Be so kind, chaps, as to raise your hands," he requested.

The lanky man with the gun took three careful steps in out of the bright morning. "The first thing you blokes are going to do," he instructed, "is tell me what sort of damage you've up and done to the Duesenberg."

"Ah, you've got us all wrong, kind sir," Groucho informed him. "We are but a pair of nature-loving vagabonds who've lost our way."

"I don't know who this young hooligan is, but you, sir, are one of the blooming Marx Brothers," accused the man who must be Truett, Ravenshaw's valet. "I can't tell you apart, but I had the extreme misfortune of sitting through one of your beastly cinema efforts once."

"Beastly, you say? That may well be the most positive critique we've ever gotten for one of our movies." Smiling, Groucho held out his hand. "Permit me to introduce myself. I'm

Hippo Marx, also known as the King of the Jungle. This open-faced lad is my cousin, Blotto Marx, who, except for a regrettable tendency to swill down moonshine, is a pillar of society and sometimes a souvenir pillow from Niagara Falls."

Truett didn't shake hands, warning, "Keep your distance, Mr. Marx. I'd hate to have to shoot you, but I'd be within my rights, since you're, the pair of you, trespassers and vandals."

"C'mon, Truett," I told him, "you aren't going to shoot anybody. Ravenshaw's in enough trouble already."

"Meaning what, sir?"

"Meaning that faking a kidnapping is a criminal offense, for one thing."

"There's nobody knows it's faked, sir."

"They will as soon as we—"

"Ah, but you blokes might just be staying in the woods for a bit, so . . . Here, what's wrong with him?"

Groucho had turned quite pale and was pressing his right hand to his chest. "Frank, I . . . Oh, Jesus . . . Give me my pills . . . Quick!"

"I don't have your medicine, Groucho," I said, sounding worried. "Remember when you had that attack last night? I gave you the bottle."

"No, that . . . that can't be . . ." His eyes rolled upward, he began shivering violently.

"What is it?" Truett, lowering his gun hand, moved up closer to the afflicted Groucho.

"His heart," I explained. With my left hand, while he was distracted, I lifted a tire iron off the small workbench next to me.

"Frank, I want Eloise to have my gold watch," Groucho was gasping, knees wobbling wildly. "You can have the chain . . . and, remember . . ." He suddenly rose up on his toes, his eyelids fluttering. Then, with a keening groan, he fell forward right into Truett.

At that same moment I jumped to a position where I could whack Truett's gun hand with the tire iron.

He howled in pain, dropping the automatic on the concrete garage floor.

While he was still howling, I spun him around and punched him several times, hard, in the chin.

He fell to his knees, passed out, and dropped down in a sprawl next to the bright yellow Duesenberg.

"Another admirable display of fisticuffs," said Groucho, straightening up and brushing at the front of his sports coat.

I was already moving toward the doorway of the garage. "Let's get the hell clear of here."

We slipped around the back of the garage and into the woods, retracing our steps.

"Who, by the way, is Eloise?" I asked as we were trotting uphill toward where we'd left my car.

"I have no idea," Groucho answered. "But if I actually owned a gold watch, I'd definitely want somebody named Eloise to have it after I was gone."

Thirty-two

They'd finished posting the big billboard advertising *The Valley of Fear* on the wall of the Mammoth studios and you could see all of Miles Ravenshaw decked out as Sherlock Holmes now.

"We should've brought along a Groucho poster to slap up," said Jane.

I stopped the car at the studio gates. "Good morning, Oscar," I said to the plump uniformed guard who'd left the tile-roofed shack to approach our car.

He looked from me to his clipboard. "You must be Mr. Marx's friend, Frank Denby," he decided. "And this pretty lady is Jane Denby."

"Exactly," I said.

"You and the missus can park in Visitors Lot B, the one right next to the softball field," Oscar told me.

"Thanks."

"Wasn't Mr. Marx supposed to be here today, too?"

I did a mild take. It was a quarter to twelve and Groucho's press conference was scheduled to start at noon. "He didn't get here yet?"

Oscar shook his head. "Not so far, no."

"Well, he's not likely to miss this event," I said.

"You never can tell with Groucho Marx." Chuckling, Oscar returned to the guard shack.

The wrought-iron gates swung open and I drove onto the Mammoth grounds.

"Groucho stopped by our place over an hour ago to pick up my artistic creations," said Jane, concern in her voice. "Where the heck did he get to?"

"Let's hope he's going to show up within the next ten minutes." I drove along the palm tree–lined street to Lot B. "Otherwise our presentation's going to fall a little flat."

"You think maybe somebody waylaid him?"

"I'd prefer to believe that isn't the reason for his not showing up."

"We should've insisted he come along in our car."

"He seemed to have some reason for driving here alone."

"Well, maybe that's why he's late."

I parked the auto between a Rolls-Royce and a gray Duesenberg. "The Ford is definitely not a successful screenwriter's car," I said, getting out to jog around and open Jane's door for her. "No wonder Lew Marker and other Hollywood moguls and tycoons laugh at my script efforts."

"They're supposed to laugh, ninny, you're writing comedies."

"True," I agreed. "We'll keep the car, then."

As we neared Soundstage 2, an elephant came thumping by down the middle of the street, led by a young man in a robe and turban.

"I keep getting it mixed up," said Jane, slowing to watch

the elephant parade by. "Is it African elephants or Indian elephants that have big floppy ears like this one?"

"Elephants that have either Tarzan or Jane riding on their backs are African elephants," I explained. "At least that applies when you're at MGM."

There was a uniformed Burbank police officer standing just outside the open soundstage doorway. He, too, had a clipboard. "Name?" he inquired.

"Frank and Jane Denby."

He scanned his typed list. "Oh, yeah, here you two are. Except it says 'Jean.'"

"That's my maiden name," said Jane.

"Is Groucho Marx inside yet?" I asked the cop.

He shook his head. "He hasn't come in this way so far."

"Oy," I observed. I took Jane by the hand and we entered the cavernous Soundstage 2.

Until you got to the 221B set, it was dimly lit and shadowy all around.

Sergeant Norment came striding up as we neared the edge of the set. He fished out his pocket watch and dangled it up toward me. "Don't tell me Marx has disappeared, too?"

"We already saw him this morning, Jack," I said. "He's en route."

"By way of San Luis Obispo?"

"He'll be here. Groucho never fails to appear if there's anything resembling an audience."

"They're fidgeting already," said the policeman. "He better make his entrance damn soon."

Quite a few folding metal chairs had been added to the furnishings of Sherlock Holmes's 221B Baker Street study. Occupying the rows of chairs were Erika Klein, a bald man I assumed must be Gunther, M. J. McLeod, Lew Marker, Guy Pope, Randell McGowan, a neat, dapper man I figured to be Professor Hoffman, Victoria St. John, Nan Sommerville, the Astounding Zanzibar, Isobel Glidden, and Randy Grothkopf, who was a small sun-browned man with a head of not quite believable russet hair.

Gil Lumbard of the *Hollywood Citizen-News* and Dan Bockman from the *L.A. Times* were sitting in chairs in the first row, looking around and taking notes. Lumbard gave me a lazy salute when he saw Jane and me taking chairs in the back row. Norm Lenzer from the *Herald-Examiner* was squatting beside the armchair that Felix Denker had been murdered in. He seemed to be fascinated by the cushion. There were three newspaper photographers standing at the edge of the set, plus a photographer I was pretty sure worked for *Motion Picture* magazine now. Sitting cross-legged on a dolly was the little guy who was a legman for Johnny Whistler.

Our chairs were near Holmes's chemistry workbench. I noticed that somebody had left an empty potato chip bag next to the detective's Bunsen burner.

"I certainly want to help the police in every way I can to track down the murderer of my good friend," said Guy Pope. "But my dear Alma grows very nervous when I'm away from Merlinwood for too long, Sergeant."

"We'll be starting any minute now," I said, my voice sounding a little shaky. The way it had sounded back in high school when I was called on to answer a question I really didn't know the answer to.

The old swashbuckler glanced over at me, a frown touching his handsome face. "Do I know you, young fellow?"

"I'm Frank Denby, Groucho's associate."

"And a bigger pain in the patootie than even Groucho is," added Grothkopf. "Just another showboat who actually doesn't know his backside from his elbow."

"I bet I do," I began. "When I—"

"Neither the time nor the place for that," cautioned Jane, tugging at my coat sleeve.

"Frank is not a showboat at all," said Victoria St. John, "if I might put my two cents' worth in, although I've never quite comprehended that expression, despite the fact that I had a very good and thorough education, or why we put so low a price on our honest opinions, unless perhaps it derives from some custom in old England, but even there, where it would probably have been twopence worth instead of two cents', that can't have been a large sum, except to people who may've been devastated by the—"

"Get to the point," the publicity man urged Victoria.

"I was merely defending Frank Denby's character, Mr. Grothkopf," she said. "And I must say that someone with such a fictitious-looking head of hair really ought not to be calling the kettle—"

"Ah, the chimes are striking high noon," said Groucho, coming in through the door next to Sherlock Holmes's desk. "Time to begin our little private inquest."

He was wearing an Inverness cape over his tweedy sports coat and had a Holmesian deerstalker cap on his head at a slightly skewed angle. Tucked up under his arm was a scruffed black attaché case with a few battered travel stickers from South American hotels slapped on its sides.

All four photographers started snapping pictures and flashbulbs flashed.

"You didn't come in through the studio gate," I said.

"I did not, Rollo, no."

"Then how'd you get in here?"

He set the case on Holmes's desk with a smack. "The same way the killer did the other night," he said. "I wanted to see if I could do it, too. And I did."

Thirty-three

Shedding the cape, Groucho hung it carefully on Sherlock Holmes's coat rack. He took off the deerstalker, tossed that onto the desk. "Before we get to the murder of Felix Denker," he announced, "there are a few other items to take care of."

"Don't tell me," said the scowling Grothkopf, "that you're going to sing first?"

"No, fear not, I didn't bring my mandolin."

"You don't play the mandolin."

"Yet another reason for leaving it home." Groucho hoisted himself up and sat on the edge of the detective's desk, legs dangling. His socks didn't match, one being green-and-white checks and the other a yellow-and-red argyle. "There has been, thanks to the noble efforts of the Mammoth publicity machine, considerable discussion in the press about a challenge issued by Miles Ravenshaw, hereinafter referred to as the hambone of the first part, to myself and my associate, Frank Denby. The fact that Ravenshaw was portraying none other than Sherlock Holmes on the silver screen apparently addled his wits, persuading him he had some talent for the solving of mysteries. He was, however, woefully—"

"Miles used to be a Scotland Yard inspector," said the publicity man loudly. "He, unlike you, Groucho, had professional experience in criminal investigation and—"

"The only firsthand experience Ravenshaw ever had with police work was when he got a ticket for double-parking his Duesenberg on Rodeo Drive last summer." He opened the attaché case and took out his legal pad. "After being sacked as a bookshop clerk in London for allegedly pilfering from the cash register, Ravenshaw became a touring actor and inflicted his modest talent on the provinces until he landed a few bit parts in the West End. From there it was into the cinema and finally Hollywood. At no time during the whole shabby odyssey was Ravenshaw ever connected with Scotland Yard. His entire career as a police inspector is moonshine brewed by Grothkopf and associates."

"That's ridiculous, it's nonsense," charged Grothkopf, standing up. "Miles Ravenshaw's record with Scotland Yard is—"

"Can you show us a copy of that record, Randy?" asked Bockman.

"I don't have the actual documentation, no, but to question a man of Miles Ravenshaw's obvious integrity is—"

"In my vaudeville days," mentioned Groucho, "hecklers were often tossed out into the alley. If you keep intruding in my discourse, Grothkopf, I'll have to ask the bobbies to give you the old heave-ho."

Lumbard asked him, "You can prove what you're saying about Ravenshaw?"

"I'll give you a list of my sources after my lecture," promised Groucho. "Now, while we're still dwelling on the topic of

Ravenshaw, let's turn to *The Mystery of the Missing Ham*. Frank, do you have that woodland address handy?"

I'd memorized the address of the cabin where Ravenshaw, Truett, and the disabled Duesenberg were languishing. "Yeah," I said, and recited it.

"Anyone dropping in at that rustic locale," suggested Groucho, "will find Ravenshaw."

Lenzer asked, "You're saying that's where the kidnappers took the guy?"

"I'm saying, Norman, that that's where Ravenshaw took himself to avoid having to admit that he was no closer to solving the case than he had been the day he started," answered Groucho. "The abduction was another publicity gimmick, designed to keep Ravenshaw's name in the news and at the same time get him off the hook."

"I've heard about enough of this crap." Grothkopf, fists clenched, stood up again. "You can't stand there, Groucho, and say that a decent and respected—"

"Here's something else I'm going to say," he cut in. "You and Ravenshaw rigged the whole thing. I'm stating this in front of witnesses, Grothkopf, and if you believe I'm lying, sue me for slander. Otherwise, sit down and cease your prattling."

"They got you on this one, good and proper," Mary Jane told her boss. "Don't make it worse."

From the edge of the set Sergeant Norment said, "Faking a kidnapping is a lot more serious than getting a parking ticket, Grothkopf."

"I don't know a damn thing about that," insisted the publicity man. "If Miles took it upon himself to stage a phony—"

"Can I have that address again, Frank?" the sergeant requested.

"Sure." I gave it to him.

"Siegel, get in touch with the Santa Barbara police, ask them to check on this."

Somewhat subdued, Grothkopf sat down.

Lighting a cigarette, Sergeant Norment eyed Groucho. "Have you ever, Marx, heard of something called withholding evidence?"

"I'm not withholding a thing, Sarge," he said, spreading his arms wide and assuming a guileless expression. "The whole purpose of this press conference is to unload everything we know on the world. I'm even prepared to reveal my shirt and shoe sizes."

The cop blew out smoke and said nothing.

Groucho left the desk to wander over to a large steamer trunk that was sitting on the bearskin rug. He perched atop it.

I leaned close to Jane. "Groucho managed to round up a pretty impressive trunk," I whispered.

Groucho cleared his throat importantly. "What we're dealing with is not one murder but two," Groucho began, holding up two fingers. "The first one has thus far been written off as an accident, but—"

"Who was murdered?" asked Bockman of the *Times*.

"A young woman named Marsha Tederow," answered Groucho. "She worked right here at Mammoth as an art director. She was also very romantically involved with Felix Denker."

"Please, Groucho," requested Erika Klein softly. "There's really no need to smear poor Felix's memory by bringing up his unfortunate tendency to—"

"Ah, but there is," countered Groucho. "Because if Marsha hadn't been having an affair with your husband, she never would have found out about Dr. Helga Krieger."

"Who?" asked Lumbard.

"Spell that," said Lenzer.

While Groucho was spelling the name, Sergeant Norment moved onto the 221B Baker Street set. He walked over and seated himself in Dr. Watson's armchair. "Go on, Marx," he said.

Groucho told them about Dr. Helga Krieger, explaining that she was a dedicated Nazi who'd dropped from sight in Germany in the early 1930s and that she'd been picked by the Hitler espionage system to be smuggled into America with a new face and a new identity. "Felix Denker was involved in that business," added Groucho, "which is why he was killed."

"This is a ridiculous travesty," said Erika, angry. "You're completely fabricating a—"

"What identity did this Nazi dame assume?" Bockman asked.

Pointing at Professor Hoffman, Groucho asked, "Did you round up a copy of *The Superiority of the Aryan Race*, Ernie?"

"Yes, right here." The professor opened a briefcase and extracted a copy of the book I'd seen, briefly, at the San Amaro love nest. He passed it to Groucho.

"This was a popular book with the beer hall crowd." Groucho opened the hardcover book to the photograph of Helga Krieger. "This is what the good doctor looked like before a very extensive face-lift and a drastic diet."

Bockman stood up, squinted at the picture. "Doesn't look like anybody I know."

Groucho closed the book and returned to the desk. From out of the well-worn attaché case he lifted several pages of Photostats. "Felix Denker started keeping a journal back in the 1920s in his native Germany," he said. "When he came to

America he brought the volumes of his journal with him, as well as some copies of Dr. Krieger's anti-Semitic works. He kept all this material carefully hidden, figuring he might have use for it someday."

"I know of no such journals," said Erika.

"But you do, dear lady," said Groucho. "You had your goons hunt for them at Denker's mansion and at the hideaway he sometimes shared with Marsha and at the house she lived in with Victoria St. John."

Lenzer frowned at him. "What exactly are you hinting about the widow, Groucho?"

"Not hinting, my boy, stating flat out that Erika Klein and Helga Krieger are one, and the same and that Felix Denker was paid a tidy sum to marry her and help her slip into the country."

"Enough!" Erika rose up. "I shall not remain here and listen to this jackanapes spew lies and—"

"Actually, ma'am, you'd better stick around," advised Norment. "Boys, see that Mrs. Denker doesn't exit just yet. Go on, Groucho."

"We haven't found the journals either," Groucho admitted, holding up the stats.

Jane whispered, "They look pretty authentic, don't they?"

I patted her hand. "From here at least. You did a good job."

"But, thanks to Victoria, we did locate the copies that Marsha Tederow made of certain significant entries." He shuffled through the pages, selected one, and dropped the others back into the case. "We've had these studied by a handwriting expert and they are positively in the handwriting of Felix Denker. With the help of Professor Hoffman, I've been able to prepare an English translation." He lifted a sheet of typing paper out of the attaché case. "Keep in mind that this is a very rough and quickly prepared translation. There was no date on this particular page." He cleared his throat again. "Here's what Denker had to say. 'It's a terrible thing I am doing, violating my beliefs and what I thought I stood for. Yet, I fear, I have no choice. The gamblers will surely kill me unless I can find some way to pay them very soon and the Nazis are offering me enough cash to settle all my debts and get out from under this terrible burden.' And then at the bottom of the page he says, 'Helga Krieger is someone I have always despised, and even now that she has become Erika Klein, it is going to be extremely difficult to carry out this—' "

"Those are lies!" cried Erika. "My husband never wrote any such words about—"

"Suppose, Marx, you get to what you think happened here on Monday night," said Norment. "And explain how all this stuff relates to that."

Groucho nodded in my direction. "Why don't you handle that, Frank?" He returned to sit again atop the big black trunk.

Standing, I went up and took a position in front of the desk. "Okay, Denker had confided in Marsha Tederow about the true nature of his marriage and about who Erika really was." I outlined our theory, which I presented as absolute proven truth, that Marsha had decided to blackmail Erika.

"She did no such thing," said the widow.

"Randell McGowan overheard her making one such attempt," I said.

"By Jove, I did at that," exclaimed the actor. "Yes, but of course, that's exactly what it was I stumbled on to."

"Thing was, Erika had no intention of paying money to her husband's mistress," I went on. "So she had Marsha lured to a bar in Sherman Oaks called the Cutting Room. Driving home from that meeting, Marsha had her fatal car accident."

"You guys are claiming that wasn't an accident?" asked Norment.

"We are, indeed." Groucho was on his feet again. "That initial murder, the killing of Marsha Tederow, is what precipitated Denker's death."

"How?" asked Lumbard.

"Denker realized as soon as he heard about Marsha's accident," said Groucho, "that it had been arranged, and he knew who'd done it. He brooded about it for a few days, thought about confiding in his friend Professor Hoffman and then decided not to. What he finally decided to do was confront Erika. Since they no longer lived together, he set up a meeting here at the studio after hours." Groucho took a cigar out of his jacket pocket and absently unwrapped it. "I'm not certain, but I think that Denker gave Erika some kid of ultimatum. Clear out or he was going to tell everything he knew and suspected to the police and the FBI. Well, Erika couldn't have that. So she shot him."

"He was shot by someone he knew," I added. "And apparently he wasn't expecting it."

Erika's laugh was harsh. "A pair of unsuccessful screenwriters have been spinning a shabby tale for you all," she said scornfully. "A tale full of lies and inconsistencies. Everyone knows—and Sergeant Norment has confirmed this—that I left the studio hours before poor Felix was killed."

"Let me tell you how you got back inside that night," offered Groucho. "It's the same way I arrived today. Really, it's not too difficult, since even I could accomplish it. Running all along the back wall of the Mammoth studios are tall oak trees. They're, most of them, higher than the wall, and the branches come very close to the wall's edge. What you do is climb a tree, toss a rope ladder over the wall, and climb down inside. With the help of a Mammoth stuntman my devoted brother Zeppo put me in touch with, I was able to scale the wall with ease." He took a small, modest bow. "At night, I found out, there's only one guard who patrols the whole back lot. Easy for somebody who works here to find out his schedule. So Monday, Erika, you returned to Mammoth, kept your prearranged appointment with your husband and, when he threatened to expose you, you knocked him off."

"That's why Denker was trying to draw a swastika on the magazine," I said. "To point to a hidden Nazi who—"

"Nonsense," said Erika evenly. "I certainly did not climb a high wall, nor did I kill my dear husband. And I most certainly was never in any saloon called the Cutting Room."

"No, right, you weren't," agreed Groucho. "That was Gunther."

The valet laughed quietly. "More pipe dreams, I fear, Mr. Marx," he said.

Groucho rose from the trunk. "Now, friends, the Astounding Zanzibar, one of the most gifted magicians in all of Southern California, is going to assist me with the next part of my demonstration," he announced. "You photographers had best stand by."

After patting Nan on her knee, Zanzibar made his way up to the steamer trunk. "This is a simple experiment in teleportation, ladies and—"

"This is outrageous," Erika complained. "To be accused of murdering one's own husband and then to be subjected to a tawdry carnival act."

"Nothing tawdry about Zanzibar," Groucho assured her.

"He's performed before the crowned heads of Europe, the few that were left. Please continue, maestro."

A silver-tipped wand had appeared in the magician's right hand. "We are merely going to bring our guests to Burbank from Sherman Oaks, a task of no great difficulty for anyone who has studied astral projection in the mystic regions of far-off Tibet." He waved the wand over the trunk. "Lando mistif-carum omnibus."

Green smoke began to swirl up all around the trunk.

The lid popped open with a brass gong sound.

The three midget Spiegelman Brothers leaped into view.

Leroy, the short, redheaded one, noticed Gunther first. "There's the man," he said, pointing. "He's the cowboy who met with Marsha Tederow at the Cutting Room that night."

"Yeah, that's him," seconded a brother, jabbing a finger in the bald valet's direction. "Minus the rug and the drugstore cowboy outfit."

Gunther's hand slid inside his jacket and he came to his feet holding a .32 revolver. "Enough of this," he said. "Erika, you and I will leave now."

"Idiot," she told him, not moving. "This was all a bluff. These fools couldn't have proven a—"

"We'll go." Gunther grabbed her arm with his free hand, yanked her to her feet.

Norment said, "Okay, boys."

All the overhead lights blossomed brightly.

Up above on the catwalk were stationed two uniformed officers with rifles.

"They'll pop you off before you can get off a shot," Norment told the bald valet. "Of course, you're welcome to give it a try."

"No, I think not." Carefully Gunther bent and put the gun on the floor and then moved away from it.

Groucho had time to say, "It worked pretty well, Rollo," before the reporters surrounded him. The photographers alternated between taking pictures of Erika and Gunther as they were handcuffed and led away and Groucho.

After several requests, Groucho agreed to pose for some pictures wearing the Sherlock Holmes hat.

I worked my way back to Jane's side and put my arm around her. "Your career as a forger got off to a nice start," I said.

"It was the Spiegelman Brothers who really—"

"Hi, Janey," said Leroy, hugging her around the knees. "Wasn't that a terrific entrance we made? We're thinking of teaming up with this Zanzibar guy and touring the supper clubs."

Someone tapped me on the arm.

It was Lew Marker, the producer. "Say, listen," he said. "If you and Groucho can add a murder to that bus idea of yours, I think we can definitely talk a deal."

Thirty-four

It was a warm, sunny December Saturday morning. Jane and I were finishing up decorating our Christmas tree.

She was standing on a low three-legged stool, wearing white slacks and a dark blue pullover. When she stretched up to affix the handmade star to the tip of the tree, the sweater hiked up, showing about three inches of her smooth tan back.

"You're sure this tree isn't too tall?" she asked, glancing down at me.

I was festooning the lower branches with silvery tinsel. "This is our first Christmas tree as a married couple," I reminded her. "And a five-foot tree isn't, technically, a forest giant anyway."

"Well, that's the way I felt while I was roaming the tree lot. This is a special occasion and so we need something fairly tall."

"Also keep in mind," I added, "that as the first tree of our married life, it automatically becomes part of family lore and legend. We'll glue snapshots of it in our photo album, we'll show them to our children in years to come, spinning tales of this historical Yuletide season. They'll pass those pictures and stories on to their children and by the time a few generations have come and gone everybody even remotely related to us will be completely and thoroughly bored with this damned tree."

"Stop eating the popcorn," Jane advised, stepping down from the stool. "It's for stringing."

I removed my hand from the big red bowl of freshly popped popcorn. "You keep treating poor waifs like this and you'll be visited by a trio of ghosts come midnight."

"I sure hope they're the ghosts of old sailors. Sailors are always a lot of fun."

Setting the bowl on our coffee table, I took a few steps back to study the tree. "That's a splendid star you created," I observed. "And those cherubs you designed, cut out, and stuck up all over the tree are charming."

"Your tinsel is droopy," she said. "But I suppose that isn't your fault. Not every man can fling tinsel in such a way that—"

"How about a stroll along the beach before lunch?"

Jane was standing with her right hand clasping her elbow and her left hand cupping her chin, left hip out-thrust. She was scrutinizing the tree. "Remind me to tell you sometime about the year my father fell into our Christmas tree," she said. "It's not a funny story, though."

"The stroll?"

"Let me freshen up and grab a sweater," she said. "Meet you down there."

"It's a date, mum." I put on a windbreaker and went trotting down to the edge of the sea.

There was another abandoned sand castle there, larger and more intricate than the last one. I had no idea who was building them.

In the castle's courtyard this time stood two lead soldiers in what looked to be British army uniforms. Both of them wore gas masks.

I left them there and walked a short distance along the wet sand.

The gulls were circling high up today, gliding soundlessly.

I seated myself on a large, smooth chunk of driftwood. I picked up a small twist of purplish seaweed, wound it around my wrist a few times, and then tossed it away among the pebbles and seashells. It smelled strongly of salt water and iodine.

"The object of a stroll is to keep moving." Jane was standing beside me, wide-legged and hands on hips. "Exercise, too, requires motion and not sitting on your duff."

I got up slowly. "Our first married Christmas is going to be okay," I decided as we walked along near the surf.

"Do me a favor, Frank."

"Anything, my love, so long as it doesn't involve a large outlay of cash."

"No, seriously." She took my hand, frowning.

"Okay, I'll be serious," I promised. "Although I can't say how long that will last."

"I'd prefer that you didn't talk so much about how happy we are or what a swell life we have. Okay?"

"Okay, sure, but—"

"I get scared, is all. I'm happy myself, but sometimes . . . I don't know, there's going to be a war and maybe everything we have will just get taken away."

"That won't happen."

She stopped, put her arms tight around me, and kissed me. "That's enough serious stuff for today," she said quietly, smiling.

"I know what you're talking about, Jane, and—"

From behind us an odd combination of snuffling, barking, and yelping had commenced.

I turned to look back.

Running right for us, in his slightly waddling way, was a bloodhound with a lolling tongue.

"That's Dorgan, isn't it?" said Jane, laughing and squatting on the sand.

The dog came running up to her. He put his front paws on her knees and started licking her face.

"It's Dorgan, sure enough," I said.

Leaving Jane, the dog came over to me. He rose up on his hind legs, pushed his forepaws into my groin, and barked with enthusiasm. "Dorgan, what brings you to Bayside?" I asked, rubbing at his knobby head.

Jane stood. "It can't be that Groucho has another case for you to work on so soon," she said.

"Here, here, don't look a gift hound in the mouth." Groucho, wearing a pair of tree green slacks, a tweedy sports coat, and a polo shirt of Santa Claus red, was hurrying toward us in a bent-knee stride.

"Wait a minute." Jane eyed him. "What was that about a gift?"

He sighed. "I knew I should have had him gift-wrapped, but there was such a line that—"

"You're giving us Dorgan?" I asked.

The dog had returned to Jane and was lying on his back at her feet. She crouched, rubbing his gray stomach again. "But he must be a very expensive dog, Groucho, what with his work in the movies and all."

"When Rollo mentioned, during our recent safari to the

remote regions of darkest Santa Barbara, that you two doted on this creature and actually had voted him more personable and sweeter-smelling than me, it struck me that he would make the ideal Christmas present. Mind you, I came to that conclusion before I'd had the paltry gift you gave me x-rayed or appraised by a team of expert pawnbrokers who specialize in—"

"He's a great present, Groucho," said Jane. "I didn't mean to harp on the cost, but—"

"As it turns out, Dorgan—and, alas, this happens to many of us in the cinema trade—is getting a bit long in the tooth— and even longer in the tongue, if you ask me—and his master has been thinking seriously of retiring the noble fellow to some old hounds home," explained Groucho. "Therefore I was able to acquire Dorgan's services at a bargain price. And you should have realized, children, that if he hadn't been on sale, you'd have gotten the usual bottle of pickled onions that I give to everybody else on my gift list during this festive season."

Jane left off rubbing Dorgan's belly and stood up again. She kissed Groucho on the cheek. "I know you hate to hear this," she told him. "But you can be a very nice man."

"Be careful you don't ever say that in front of witnesses," he warned. "Oh, and Dorgan has all the necessary licenses and tags and shots. He's also housebroken, which is more than I can say for myself."

"Thanks," I said. "This brightens our holiday considerably, Groucho."

"Come on up to the house," invited Jane, "and see our Christmas tree."

"I will," said Groucho. "And, as Tiny Tim observed, 'Who stole my crutch?' "